KEREN DAVID

CUCKOO

ATOM

ATOM

First published in Great Britain in 2016 by Atom

1 3 5 7 9 10 8 6 4 2

A CIP catalogue record for this book
is available from the British Library.

ISBN 978-0-349-00235-4

Typeset in Palatino by M Rules
Printed and bound in Great Britain by
Clays Ltd, St Ives plc

Papers used by Atom are from well-managed forests
and other responsible sources.

Remembering our brilliant friend
Dolly Bloggs,
always utterly true to himself.

For his family, Candy, Tiger,
Hector and Sylvester,
with much love.

PART 1

And let me speak to th' yet-unknowing world
How these things came about.

Hamlet, Act 5, scene 2.

EPISODE 1

Jake Benn, face to camera. He's sitting on a dark wood floor, leaning against a bed.

He speaks. His voice is soft and nervous, yet still easy to listen to.

'I'm sorry.

'I know a lot of people are upset, right now, angry with me and my family. You're probably one of those people. You need someone to blame and I'm that person. Me and my dad. You hate us.

'*Market Square* was so popular. Not just here in Britain either; they sold it all around the world. Millions watched it. It won the Best Soap award, year after year. It'd been on television for more than thirty years.

'I can't believe they cancelled it. No more *Market*

Square. It's unthinkable, like draining the River Thames and building a motorway there instead. Or painting all the red buses green, or turning the Houses of Parliament into a bowling alley.

'I don't think I'm exaggerating. They even discussed it on *Newsnight*.'

Evan Davis in the Newsnight studio, flanked by a man and a woman.

'A soap opera closes, a nation mourns. Losing Market Square, some say, is an assault on the British way of life. Here to discuss the shocking end of a drama that has kept fans entertained for more than thirty years is Market Square's former editor, Marcus Remington, and cultural commentator and newspaper columnist Miranda Shah.'

'So I do get it and believe me I feel guilty.

'My agent keeps telling me that it's not my fault. The cast, they've been kind about what happened. Mostly. Mum's very upset, but we're supporting each other.

'I've been trying to work out why Dad ... why Kirsty ... why everyone did what they did. But it's not that easy to understand. You can't tell the whole story in a statement to the media.

'So I had an idea. I thought, I'll tell the story on the Internet, bit by bit, and I'll make it as accurate as I can.

'I'm going to recreate actual events, and let people talk

for themselves. Of course, some people won't, or can't. Dad, for example; he's not in a good place right now. Adam ... Marguerite ...

'But when people can, they will. We'll act the rest of it. I know loads of actors, and most of them are out of work – sorry, guys – so I've got people helping me out.

'It's not just about *Market Square*. I've got important stuff to say, about things that have happened to me, people I've met. Things that are a lot more important than a soap getting cancelled. I'm not saying that the show didn't matter. I know a lot of people love television. For a lot of fans *Market Square* was their family, their community, their world. If that's you, I'm sorry. But there is other stuff that matters too. Real life. Real people.

'My story ... there are bits of it ... it's more dramatic than you'd think. Some of it has been in the papers, but not the whole thing. Not half of it.

'It's not going to be easy to talk about some parts, but it's my way of trying to make up for the show getting cancelled. I'm going to ... this is me making my own drama series, with help from a lot of friends.

'It won't be *Market Square*, of course, but it'll be something.

'I could begin when I was six and I got my first ever professional acting job, in an advert for fish fingers. Or maybe when I was twelve, four years ago, and I got the part on *Market Square*. I was Riley Elliott, and the Elliott family had just moved onto the Square. My dad was

Freddie Elliott, car mechanic and drug dealer. My mum
ran a fruit and veg stall. I had an older sister called Poppy
and an older brother called Mike and my first storyline
was Riley getting arrested for shoplifting.

'We Elliotts were the main family in the Square. I
know people talked about the Carpenters and the Khans,
but who had the strongest storylines? We did! And Riley
was totally a part of it.

'I loved it. It was great having a part that didn't stop –
not like the films and TV I'd done before. I was Riley and
Riley was me and his life went on alongside mine. I got
to work with a great bunch of people, and I wasn't just
a schoolkid, I was a professional actor, with colleagues.

'And I didn't have to go to many auditions anymore.

'I won Best Newcomer at the National Soap Awards.
I had – have – a fan club; they call themselves Riley's
Angels. I fronted a national campaign on knife crime,
when Riley got involved with that gang. I've had mas-
sively strong storylines. People loved me. I mean Riley.
They loved him.

'It was a shock when Marcus, the editor, said Riley
was having a bit of a rest, and when they sent him to his
room and just left him out of the scripts. They wouldn't
negotiate a new contract with my agent. "Let's wait
and see," they said. "We'll decide where the character's
going."

'It wasn't easy waiting for them to decide. People
were making jokes about what Riley was doing in his

bedroom, and what he'd look like when he came out. There were all sorts of rumours about who might become Riley, and no one seemed to think that he'd still be me.

'It was stressful, and undermining, and ... and it would've been easier if they'd just killed Riley off – a house fire maybe, or a virus, a kidnap. I got quite good at dreaming up ways they could put us both out of our misery. But they didn't. So every time I went to an audition there were questions about my availability. Questions that no one could answer. And there were comments about typecasting. My branding. "The boy off *Market Square.*" Whether I'd be going back.

'I couldn't be Riley, and yet I couldn't not be him, if you see what I mean.

'There aren't that many parts for fifteen- and sixteen-year-olds. It's a difficult age. We're not little ragamuffins anymore, and it's easy to find adult actors who look young enough to be us. A lot of people I used to see on the audition circuit had disappeared. They'd all started concentrating on exams and university and their future.

'I only want to be an actor. I'm hoping that this, what happened, won't ruin my career.

'I'll put another video up on Thursday. It'll be about an audition I did, nine months after they sent Riley to his bedroom.

'I still don't know why they did that.'

Click to see previous comments

MarketSquareFan Do you think any apology can ever be enough for getting our beloved show cancelled? You are so arrogant, you take my breath away. Of course they sacked you. You were rubbish. Don't think there's anything you can do to make up for what your family did.

Tammi♥Jake OMG, this is AMAZING. Thank you so much! Am I going to be in it?

Robster Who cares? *Market Square* was a crappy soap. Let it go.

MarketSquareFan For some of us, *Market Square* was a way of life. My mum lived and breathed *Market Square*. In her last years the characters were more real to her than her own family. And now they're not there anymore.

LizzieK Can someone just tell me – did Amina go off with her boyfriend? Or did the arranged marriage go through? Can't stop thinking about it.

Robster Get a life, MarketSquareFan. You and your mum.

MarketSquareFan As Mum passed away a month ago, I find that very offensive. And now she'll never know about Amina either.

Click to load more comments

8

EPISODE 2

Jake Benn and Dylan Johnson are sitting on two chairs against a plain white wall.

'You nervous, Jake?'

'Not really. You?'

'Yeah, I'm always nervous. It's good, I think. Gets the adrenaline up.'

'I've done a course about eliminating audition nerves. Breathing and stuff. Mindfulness.'

Jake demonstrates the breathing technique.

'Yeah, been there, done that. I still prefer to feel it; you know? Clammy hands, sick feeling in my stomach.

Throat drying out, heart beating just that little bit faster. Makes it more real. When I auditioned for Simon Steinberg, I threw up beforehand. Maybe that's what made the difference.'

'Wondered when you'd drop Simon Steinberg's name into the conversation. Took you five minutes, that's a personal best, Dylan.'

'Can I help it that I got picked by a genuine Hollywood director for that *Young Sherlock* thing? Admit it, mate, you're jealous.'

'Not actually picked for Sherlock though.'

'Obviously they had to have an American for that. Noah Blaskett did a brilliant job. I might go out to Hollywood to see him in the summer; he's a really good friend now.'

'Unless you get this job. They said filming would be this summer.'

'Actually, they said May or June, which is a pain because of GCSEs. But I'm hoping the schedule will fit around the exams.'

'I'm just assuming I'll be free. I don't care about GCSEs, but they still haven't said about *Market Square*.'

'How long's it been now?'

'Nine months.'

'Whoah. But they haven't said that they've dumped you?'

'My agent's talking to them, seeing what they'll offer. I've got quite a following.'

'You sure have. Ten thousand followers on Twitter, eh?'

'Yeah, something like that.'

'Got that blue tick.'

'Yeah. Don't tweet often. Not enough, really. My agent says I should be tweeting every day. But I don't really know what to say.'

'Just small stuff. Link to your Instagram. Noah has five million followers.'

'Wow.'

'He has an assistant who tweets for him.'

'Does he like that?'

'He says it's safer that way.'

'Is that all the assistant does?'

'No, obviously; he does all Noah's social media. And fanmail. Full time job.'

'My grandma used to do all my fan stuff – sending out pictures and answering letters. She liked doing it.'

'I'm sorry about your grandma, man. She used to love coming to stuff like this, didn't she? Auditions and rehearsals and shoots.'

'Yeah.'

There's a short, painful pause.

'So, what do you make of this role then, Jake? Learned your pages?'

'Yeah, absolutely. I thought I'd just read it. Don't want to look desperate.'

'Confidence. That's what this part is all about. Got to go in there looking like you believe you've been born to rule.'

'Yeah, although Prince Jasper is vulnerable. I mean, he loses the battle, doesn't he? Gets taken prisoner.'

'Vulnerable? Interesting interpretation, Jakey-boy. A brave choice. Because it's not there in the script, is it?'

'Well, I suppose it depends how you read it.'

'I just don't see it.'

'The bit . . . the bit where he's asking for their support? I thought there could be something there.'

'I would've thought that's when he needs to be at his most confident. Regal. After all, if they think he's a complete wuss, he's lost the battle before it starts. Think Shakespeare. Think Agincourt.'

'Yeah. Maybe you're right, Dylan.'

Jake wipes his hands on his jeans. Dylan smiles.

'Jake Benn? We'll see you now.'

'Good luck, Jakey-boy. May the best man win.'

Click to see previous comments

LillyM Dylan Johnson's going to be in this? I LOVE DYLAN.

Melaneeee I remember when you two were in that

CUCKOO

film together. The one with the zookeeper. OMG, you were so cute.

    MarketSquareFan I thought this was going to explain what happened with *Market Square*? Get on with it.

Click to load more comments

EPISODE 3

*Jake and his dad, Neil, are in the car going home
from the audition. Neil's forehead is furrowed, and
his mouth is a grim line. He's tapping his hand
impatiently against the steering wheel.*

'So? How did it go? Don't keep me in suspense.'

'Alright, I suppose.'

'Alright? Just alright? Alright good or alright disaster?'

'Not a disaster, just difficult to tell what they thought.
It was all, "Here you go, say your stuff, goodbye, we'll let
your agent know."'

'Was the casting director there?'

'No. They taped it.'

'Oh, that's bad. I'll speak to Zoe about that.'

'Dad, I don't think there's anything Zoe can do about it.'

'Zoe's your agent. She ought to make sure you're going to auditions with actual casting directors, not being taped by some young girl straight out of college.'

'I know, but—'

'Leave it to me. In fact, why don't I call her now?'

'You're driving, Dad.'

Neil's irritated.

'Hands-free, OK, Jake?'

'No . . . it's OK. Do you want me to get the number for you?'

'Obviously. Yes.'

Jake types the number into Neil's phone, and they wait silently.

'Bryant and Bold, Kelly speaking.'

'Zoe, please.'

'Can I ask who's calling?'

'Neil. Neil Benn. Jake's dad. She'll know.'

There's a pause.

'I'm afraid Zoe's not around this afternoon. I'll ask her to call you back.'

Neil exhales, and mouths 'Liars' at the phone.

'You do that. It's urgent. I'll expect her call this afternoon.'

Jake switches the phone off.

'You can't be soft with these people, Jake. They're paid to get you work. Bloody sharks. They need to know who's boss.'

'Yes, Dad, but—'

'Don't argue, Jake. I find it very stressful, and I already have a headache. Just take it from me, I know what's what.'

'Yes. OK. It's just that—'

'That's enough!'

'OK. OK, Dad, sorry.'

'I was talking to Suzanne outside. She says Dylan's been very busy, here, there and everywhere for auditions. Might be up for something in the West End.'

'Dylan never said anything about the West End.'

'That'll be because he won't want you trying out for it too. The less competition the better. Why didn't Zoe put you up for it? Was she asleep on the job? Remind me to mention it to her.'

'Dad . . .'

'What?'

'I like Zoe. She's not going to forget me. Please, just be nice to her.'

'Come on, Jake. You've got to push yourself to the front of the queue.'

'Yeah, yeah.'

'It's important, Jake. It's not a game.'

'I know that.'

'Your agent has hundreds of kids just like you, jostling for her attention.'

'She's not going to forget about me.'

'Too right they're not. I told Zoe last time I spoke to her, "We're trusting you," I said. "Sort it out with *Market Square*. Get Jake back on screen. He's popular. He's got a following. And get him a pay rise while you're at it."'

'Dad! For God's sake.'

'I'm only thinking of you, son. She gets her cut, it's in her interest as well.'

'Look, why don't I talk to Zoe? Less stress for you.'

'Less stress for me? You're sixteen years old and you think you can manage for yourself? What a joke. I'll tell you what would be less stressful for me – if you got a job for once.'

'I know, I'm sorry. I am trying. It's just ... you know stress is bad for you. You said you had a headache.'

'I have a headache every day, worrying about your career.'

'Dad. It's not really a life or death situation.'

'You might not give a shit about your career, Jake, but it is life or death as far as I'm concerned and I'm damned if I'll sit quietly and watch it slip away from us as if it's no big deal.'

'Dad, really?'

Neil exhales and counts silently to ten.

'You're right. I'm sorry. I'm letting it get to me.'
'It's OK.'
'The whole thing. My job. Your job.'
'I know.'
'It's just that the way things are, you're more likely than me to get work.'
'Not necessarily, Dad. You're good at what you do.'
'So are lots of people. Most of them are younger and cheaper than me, and they haven't got, you know, my issues.'
'It's OK.'
'And they haven't got a kid at home to look after.'
'I know.'
'You're lucky, Jake. You're the one who's free to go away and do exciting stuff and get paid for it.'
'I know.'
'You just need that lucky break. Another lucky break.'
'It's OK. It'll happen.'
'You're our superstar, you know that?'
'Thanks, Dad.'
'We only want what's best for you.'
'Sure.'
'And it will happen. No pressure, eh?'
'No. No pressure.'

Click to see previous comments

MarketSquareFan You've got Hamza Hussain
playing your dad? Really? Your dad's a Pakistani guy of
30? What's going on?

DramaticDee Congratulations on your commitment
to age and colour-blind casting! (I've seen pictures of
your dad in the paper, so I know he's a bit older than
Hamza Hussain and definitely not a Person of Colour.)
This is so important in challenging assumptions, and
helping us reflect on White Privilege. Also, Hamza's a
great actor.

ZackAttack We've all seen pictures of your dad. He
doesn't look anything like Hamza Hussain. And if you're
going to have Hamza in your series perhaps he can tell
us if his sister's marriage was due to get called off. He
must have seen advance scripts.

JakeBenn It makes it easier for me. I mean, Hamza
can act my dad, but he's not actually my dad, which
makes it feel more like acting if you see what I mean.
Does that make sense?

DylanJohnson Lots of playwrights put themselves
in their own work, and they don't worry about it. Look at
Alan Bennett, for example. If you want, I could be you in
your series sometimes. If it gets too much.

DestinyRock Thanks for the offer, Dylan, we'll
consider it. Just a heads up, guys, in the next episode
Jake's real mum is played by Angie Rose, who most

of you know as his mum in *Market Square*. Don't get confused! She's just a great actress, and we're so grateful to have her, and obviously she and Jake are used to acting together and it just works.

MarketSquareFan So now Patsy Elliott and Tariq Khan are meant to be married? What the hell? You're just messing us about.

JakeBenn I should maybe explain that my brother's in this next episode as well. He's on the autistic spectrum. He's older than me, but seems a lot younger. You'll see.

Click to load more comments

EPISODE 4

Adam Benn is sitting on a sofa, rocking gently backwards and forwards. He is around eighteen years old, and has messy dark hair. His left thumb is in his mouth; his right hand is pulling his own hair. He is humming quietly to himself. He is watching a video of Thomas the Tank Engine.

There is a knock at the door. Adam pays no attention, but his mother rushes to open the door. Maria can be heard arguing with two men in the background. Adam finds the remote control, carefully identifies the volume button and switches the sound up.

*Maria comes into the room, accompanied by the two
men. She looks flushed, tearful, distressed. They have
professionally blank expressions.*

'Please, you can't. It's a mistake. It must be. Just wait
while I call my husband.'

**THE TROUBLESOME TRUCKS SNIGGERED
TO THEMSELVES AS THOMAS HUFFED AND
PUFFED HIS WAY ALONG THE TRACK.**

'Adam, turn that sound down! I need to call your dad.'

*The two men turn to each other. One jerks his head
towards the television. The other nods.*

'I CAN DO IT,' HUFFED THOMAS.

'Neil? Neil, can you hear me? Turn it down, Adam!
Neil, there's two men here, say they're from a collection agency. Debt collection agency. Bailiffs, yes. Turn it
down, Adam! Can you speak to them, Neil? Tell them
it's a mistake?'

*The men act at the same time. One switches the
television off, the other removes the plug from the wall.
Then they pick it up, each holding an end.*

Adam howls.

'Now look what you've done! You can't just take his Thomas away from him. He's on the spectrum. He needs his telly; put it down, please. Here ... you can have my phone.'

The men put the television down, examine the phone and shake their heads.

Enter Jake.

'What's going on?'

Adam shouts louder. He has wrapped his arms around himself and he's rocking backwards and forwards. Maria flicks tears from her eyes.

'What've you done to my mum? What are you doing to the television? My brother's autistic. You can't take his telly away from him!'

The bailiffs have recognised Jake.

'I know you, don't I? You recognise him, don't you, Brian? He's that kid off *Market Square*.'
'Little Riley! So this is where you've been.'

Both men laugh. Jake glares at them.

'Look, can you just switch the telly back on so he can watch *Thomas*? And then we can talk about this.'

'Nothing to talk about. We need to recover goods to the value of £1,400. Telly plus iPhone plus a laptop should do it.'

'There's a telly upstairs in my room. Take that one. And other stuff, too. A saxophone, two iPads . . .'

Maria dries her eyes.

'Oh, Jake, you can't . . .'
'Show them, Mum.'

The men go up the stairs and then come down again carrying Jake's television and saxophone.

'Look, what about the microwave? It's built in, but you could probably . . . or the dishwasher?'

'It's OK, Mum. I never play the sax anyway. We can get a new telly when we get all this sorted out. It's just a mix up, it must be. It is, isn't it? Don't worry.'

The bailiffs are sorting through their paperwork. One of them offers Jake a pen.

'Could I have your autograph? My daughter loves Riley.'

Maria finds her voice.

'No, no you cannot! How dare you? This is totally inappropriate.'

'Just asking, no need to get upset, love.'

'You come in our house and you take my son's stuff and then you have the cheek to ask for his autograph? Get out of here. Leave us alone!'

'Look, Mum, it's OK.'

'It is not OK! Look, my husband's on his way home. He'll sort this out. It's just a mistake. We've just had a new kitchen installed and the bills . . . it must be an oversight. You can see we've got our hands full.'

Jake's voice is calm.

'I'll sign your autograph if you promise me that this won't end up in the papers, OK?'

'If you could sign it to Carly? Carly with a "y"? We won't say anything to anyone, will we? Wouldn't want to make trouble.'

Maria is furious.

'You've already made quite enough trouble as it is. I wish you'd wait for my husband. He'll sort this out in an instant.'

'OK, here's your autograph for Carly. Now I'm going to

take a picture of you, with my brother in the background. If you tell anyone about this, then I'm going to talk to a journalist about how you bullied my disabled brother and put us through hell. It won't be nice. Carly won't like it.'

The men prepare to leave.

'OK, son. Sorry about the circumstances.'

They leave. Maria bursts into tears again. Jake gives her a hug.

'Oh, Jake, that was horrible.'

'It's OK, Mum. It's OK. Don't worry, it's going to be OK.'

'I don't understand it ... '

'Mum, it's OK. We can dip into my savings. Of course, it's difficult without my income, but you know I might get this new film. And I haven't definitely been written out of *Market Square*.'

'That's the thing, Jake. We shouldn't have to rely on you. You shouldn't be worrying about money. You're sixteen!'

'It's OK, Mum. It's OK.'

'It's not OK. I'm going to have to do more shifts at Tesco. But that'll put more strain on your dad, because it means more hours with Adam, and I don't know ... it's not good for him.'

'Don't worry, Mum. It'll work out.'
'I hope you're right, I really do.'

Click to see previous comments

ConcernedMum That was disgusting. How could
you upset that poor boy all over again, making him
relive something deeply traumatic just for the sake of
some web series? I hope social services saw it. Totally
irresponsible.

Tammi♥Jake OMG, poor Jake, that is exactly what
happened to Riley! His dad lost all their money and then
his dad shot himself! Isn't that weird and spooky?

LizzieK What if everything that happened to Riley
actually happened to Jake? How strange would that be?

Caring I completely agree with ConcernedMum about
that poor retarded boy. His mum should be strung up for
allowing him to be exploited.

DramaticDee Using the word 'retarded' is completely
offensive, and don't get me started on the connotations
of the phrase 'strung up'.

Click to load more comments

EPISODE 5

Jake's sitting on the sofa, with Adam. Adam's humming to himself, quite happily, ignoring the camera, seeming to ignore Jake.

Jake reaches out to Adam with his hand, and Adam slowly grasps it.

Jake, to camera.

'So, we got a lot of negative comments for the last episode and I thought we ought to answer them as soon as possible.

'A lot of people seemed to think that we were being cruel to Adam, making him relive the trauma of being visited by the bailiffs and everything. That it was harmful to him. That we shouldn't have used him in the film.

'The thing is, I think Adam knew what was going on. I explained it all to him beforehand. He was doing his thing where he looks up at the ceiling and hums, but when I was talking to him the humming got softer. Like this.'

Jake demonstrates. Adam joins in. The humming gets louder and louder, until Jake laughs and Adam looks away.

'That means he's listening, the humming. It's like Adam's code.

'It's really hard to explain when you don't know him. And I thought, if I got someone to act him, it'd feel like we were making fun of him.

'He always cries if the television gets switched off, and he's always fine when it goes back on again.

'But the day the bailiffs came, he was really scared. He was all shivery, his eyes were wild, and he wet himself, which he doesn't do all that often.

'None of that happened when we were filming the other day. He was fine with Angie. He knew that Logan and Dylan were only pretending to be bailiffs. He understood. I think he was trying to be an actor. It's hard to tell.

'See how he's holding my hand now? That's a huge thing for Adam. He doesn't touch many people, but he's happy, really happy to see me. I haven't seen so much of him recently because, well. We'll come to that.

'So, my mum says, those of you who offered to call social services, please don't.

'And I'm asking you to stop trolling my mum in the comments.

'Adam's OK. We're OK.

'We've got enough on our plate.'

Comments have been disabled on this episode.

EPISODE 6

Jake and his parents, Neil and Maria, are sitting at the kitchen table.

'The thing is, Jake, we can't take money from your savings.'

'You can! It's OK, I understand. It's a family crisis. You'll pay it back when you can.'

'No, Jake, listen. We can't, because ...'

Neil swallows hard.

'... because it's gone. We've already taken it. I'm so sorry.'

'You've what?'

'It was just ... I lost my job, and then Nonna died,

which meant Mum had to cut down on her shifts. We've been struggling for years.'

'You've spent my money? All of it?'

'We didn't want to worry you. We thought we could pay it back before you'd need it.'

'Pay it back with what?'

'We'd have found a way. I mean, we will find a way. It went on the mortgage. Property prices in London have gone crazy. Just a year or so and we'll re-mortgage, or even sell up.'

'But then where would we live?'

'I don't know, I just mean that money spent on a mortgage, it's not lost. We still have your money. It's in the house.'

'But ...'

'I'm sure I'll get a job eventually.'

'It's been three years, Dad.'

'You don't have to rub it in!'

'It's OK, Dad. I mean, I'm sorry. It's my fault.'

'It's not your fault, sweetheart. Neil, tell him it's not his fault. We should never have taken money from you, Jake. We're both really sorry.'

'If anyone's to blame it's that prat in charge of *Market Square*. Marcus. He should realise that people depend on him. You can't just suspend a popular character. Best Newcomer ... I feel like going down there and giving him a piece of my mind.'

'Neil! You can't do that.'

'Dad, please don't.'

'We had nothing to live on, Jake. We were mortgaged up to the hilt and then I lost my job. We've been limping along, relying on you, and then they pulled the plug and we were left high and dry.'

'I might get the Prince Jasper job. And there will be more auditions. And I can leave school very soon.'

'And that's going to help us how?'

'We won't have the fees to pay, I'll have more time for auditions and stuff, and if *Market Square* want me back I can work longer hours – they won't have to pay a tutor or a chaperone. Maybe that's what they're waiting for.'

'Love, I had to call your school and ask them about a bursary just to take you up to your exams. It's that bad.'

'Maria, no ... You didn't tell me. We'll sell up if we have to. We can't crawl to them, begging for charity. We can't!'

'Neil ...'

'Don't argue with me! I'm in control, I swear. The bailiffs, that was just a mix-up. We still have assets. But Jake is our biggest asset. You just need to get a job, son. Anything. Reality TV if necessary. I'll tell Zoe, tell her how urgent it is.'

'Dad, I'll do anything, OK? I'm really sorry about Riley. I honestly don't know what I did wrong. Let me talk to Zoe. Let me talk to Marcus. Let me—'

33

'Are you saying that I'm useless as your manager? Great, thanks, son. Good to know that you don't trust me. Really does a lot for the old self-esteem.'

'Oh, Neil, that's not fair.'

'Was it fair that I got sacked when they'd piled on the pressure and bullied me into a breakdown?'

'Neil, you hit your boss!'

'He was asking for it. And he didn't have half my experience. Jumped up idiot.'

'He was on crutches!'

'He'd only broken his leg skiing, Maria. He wasn't permanently disabled.'

'Neil.'

'Well, he wasn't before I hit him.'

Jake stands up.

'Look, I need to learn my pages for the Prince Jasper audition. That's all I can do to help.'

'It shouldn't all be on your shoulders, love. Look, Neil, there is something we can do. We could rent the house out and move somewhere cheaper. Out near my dad, maybe.'

'Essex? Grandad's home is in Dagenham. That's so far from here.'

'Only if we have to. We could find a flat, not a house. Or we could sell. We could pay you back.'

'A flat? Would I have to share a room with Adam?'

'Oh, Jake. No. We wouldn't ask that of you. Would we, Neil?'

'No. Don't worry, Jake. It won't come to that.'

'Really? You promise?'

'We promise.'

Click to see previous comments

ConcernedMum What terrible parents! Who would steal from their own child????

Caring Surely it's against the law?

FamilyMan What awful people those parents are. How can they live with themselves?

JohnfromLuton I've phoned up and reported them for theft.

Riley'sAngel Poor Jake! This is almost worse than what happened to Riley!

Tammi♥Jake Riley didn't have any money to steal.

JakeBenn Please don't troll my parents.

MarketSquareFan Can I suggest that instead of wallowing in your own problems and washing your dirty linen in public, you concentrate on telling us what happened with *Market Square*? And maybe get hold of some advance scripts and get your former colleagues to act them out? I need to know about Amina's wedding!

LizzieK I don't think they get advance scripts. Apparently there was a huge fuss a few years back when someone eavesdropped on the *Market Square* Christmas party and leaked the school explosion story.

MarketSquareFan That was a terrible storyline. Who'd believe that a head-teacher would get so wound up over a visit from inspectors?

Click to load more comments

EPISODE 7

Jake and Adam's new bedroom. Two single beds in a bare room. There are suitcases, boxes and a bin bag waiting to be unpacked. Adam's bed has a Thomas the Tank Engine *duvet, and a Thomas mobile dangling over it. On the floor there is a wooden train set.*

The noise of a Thomas the Tank Engine *video permeates through the wall.*

Jake's sitting on his bed.

'So, this is where we ended up. A crappy little flat, miles away from my school. And I did have to share a room with Adam.

'Adam and Thomas. And Henry, Edward, the Troublesome Trucks . . .

'I have to admit that I was angry. Really angry. I didn't have my work, and I didn't have any money, and I wasn't interested in school and I wasn't getting much sleep.

'I felt like my parents should have done something a lot sooner. The irony of the whole thing was how close it felt to what happened to Riley when his dad lost everything in some dodgy deal. And we all know how badly *that* turned out for the family. That suicide scene won awards, deservedly.

'That was a great storyline. It was a chance to try out being at the centre of some massive trauma, and explore all those emotions. Shock, and grief and all that. Riley went really mental for a while. He was fighting and all that. He got involved with that gang. It was brilliant, I loved it.

'But this was real life, and I didn't like it at all.

'Adam sings in the night and gets up and cries and picks up stuff that's not his and just destroys it for the sake of it. And he smells. He sweats a lot, and he hates being washed.

'And I was always stepping on his train set, which was bloody painful, but he's the one who cries about it.

'I had to take two buses and two trains to get to school. All of them stinking of sweaty armpits. And sometimes people recognised me, and took pictures with their phones and asked me for selfies, which was crap.

'But it was even more crap when no one recognised me at all.

'And that was most days.

'I felt angry all the time. I didn't feel like myself. How could I feel like this about Adam, who never hurt anyone, who just liked watching *Thomas* – bloody *Thomas* – all day? And my dad had become someone I didn't recognise. Someone I hated. I was used to all his stress, but this was different. He wasn't himself and I wasn't myself and sometimes I felt as though I was going mad.

'The one good thing was that I'd got the callback for Prince Jasper. Dylan had too. But there was no chance to work on my pages, no time or space or quiet.

'I was jealous of Dylan. I knew he'd be preparing in his huge room, in his massive house, with earphones and a laptop and a voice coach and whatever he needs. I hated Dylan. And he'd been my friend ever since we were six and we were in a commercial together for granary bread. We were Victorian children in an old-fashioned orphanage.

'The only thing going in my favour for the audition was motivation. Prince Jasper was a prisoner. And I felt like a prisoner. I could use that. I lay on this bed and pretended it was in a cell. I couldn't concentrate on the words, but I could *be* Prince Jasper.

'Even though he'd morphed into a prince who was forced to listen to sodding *Thomas the Tank Engine* all day long.

'I always thought I was basically a nice person.

'I soon discovered that was just surface.

'Beneath it was all this darkness, all this bitterness and anger, and I had no idea what to do with it at all.'

Click to see previous comments

MariaBenn I just want to say it's OK for all of you, looking in, judging. You don't know what it's been like. Jake isn't telling the whole story. It's not his fault, there's too much to tell. You haven't seen me on the tills at Tesco, working all hours for minimum wage. You haven't seen Neil trying and trying to get another job in Human Resources. You haven't seen us lying in bed, worrying. Because Jake didn't even know about all that. You try and protect your kids, don't you?

We lost my mum about a year before all this happened. She dropped dead of a heart attack. She used to be Jake's chaperone, went with him to all his auditions and everything. She helped me out with Adam, too. Since she died, it's been so hard. We've struggled with everything. My dad's had to go into a home. It's heart-breaking, it really is.

I'm trying to understand why Jake feels he needs to make this series. He's being very mysterious about it, him and that Destiny. I want to back him, support him. But I can't take all the nastiness. Someone shouted at me when I was on the till at Tescos the other day.

I've had eighteen years of looking after a child with severe special needs. I've supported my husband through a lot. I'm just an ordinary woman, doing her best to keep her family going.

Have some kindness, please.

Click to load more comments

EPISODE 8

Kirsty Connor's flat in West Hampstead, an upmarket area of London. Kirsty's having a night in with a pizza and a bottle of wine.

Kirsty's entry phone buzzes. She's not pleased to be interrupted. She pauses her film and answers.

'Hello? Who is it?'

'Kirsty? It's me, Jake.'

'Jake?'

'Yes, me, Jake. Riley! I should have rung, I know.'

'Jake? What are you doing here? OK, I'm buzzing you in.'

Jake enters, looking embarrassed.

'I should've rung or texted or something. Sorry.'
'Oh no, it's me that should say sorry, darling. Of course I knew who it was!'

Kirsty kisses Jake on the cheek.

'How's my little brother? I'm missing you on set.'
'Not going to kid you, Kirsty, everything is crap.'
'Everything?'
'Yeah. Everything.'
'Sit down and have a glass of wine and tell me all about it, darling.'

She pours Jake a large glass of wine.

'Pizza? It's a bit cold, but completely edible. Loads left over. I'm being good. Well, semi good. Poppy's about to get pregnant so I can indulge a bit.'
'Poppy's getting pregnant?'
'One-night stand. No one knows who the father is. Total cliché. Been done a million times before. I'm all set for nine months of slut-shaming. Poor old Poppy.'
'If Poppy's pregnant they've got to let Riley come downstairs, don't you think? He's the uncle after all.'
'Who knows, sweetie?'
'You do, don't you? You know something?'

'I don't know anything for sure, but I can't lie to you. Rumour has it that they want a different Riley. I'm sorry, Jake. They're talking to Bobby Broadbent.'

'But he's not an actor. He's a reality star!'

'He's a talentless git, yes.'

'He's your ex!'

'I know. I'm sorry, hon. I think that's why they're talking to him.'

'What?'

'It's a story, you see. Can they work together? Will Bobby and Kirsty get together again as brother and sister? You can see why they might consider it.'

'It's just stupid. He doesn't look anything like me.'

'Dye his hair, put him on a diet . . . that'll be tough for him, he's a greedy pig.'

'I just can't even—'

'It'd be a publicity coup. Imagine. Anyway, I'm surprised it hasn't hit the papers yet. Sorry, love.'

'It's not fair, Kirsty. It's not.'

'Help yourself to more wine, sweetie. I know, it's not. But that's the way it goes. We're just their puppets. Poppy may be shagging around and getting up the duff now, but she could die in childbirth, or in a mugging, or be murdered by the anonymous father of her baby. That's soaps. That's life.'

'Yeah, tell me about it.'

'Look, it's not necessarily a bad thing if you move on from *Market Square*. You don't want to get typecast. You don't want to end up playing Riley all your life. Look at me. All those years at drama school, learning to sing and dance, not just act. Learning Shakespeare and Sheridan and Sondheim.'

'Sondheim?'

'Famous writer of musicals, duh. And now all I do is flirt and gossip as Poppy bleeding Elliott.'

'Why don't you quit then?'

'Why do you think? Money.'

'Yeah, well, I don't have any money anymore.'

'That's just because you're a schoolkid, Jake. Your parents will be saving it up for when you leave school.'

'Nope, they spent it all. On the mortgage and school fees and a new bloody kitchen and stuff. And now we live in Essex – seriously, it's like travelling back in time out there – and I have to share a room with my brother who, it's not his fault, but he smells, and he's noisy and his toys are all over the floor.'

'Oh, Jake. He's just a baby.'

'Kirsty. He's eighteen. He's severely autistic.'

'Oh. Oh, OK, I didn't know. Jesus, Jake, that's awful. Sounds worse than being part of the Elliott family.'

'It's all just rubbish.'

'Oh, Jake, sweetie, I'm sorry. Have some more wine.'

'I'm just . . . it's all a mess, Kirsty. I'm a mess. And now I've got a callback, and it's really important, and I've got nowhere to read or practise, and at school all they care about is stupid exams . . .'

'Jake, darling, try not to spill the wine. OK, let me take it. I think you've had enough. OK, lie down on the sofa. That's good. I think you'd better sleep here.'

'But I . . . I can't.'

'I could call you a cab. But you're a bit the worse for wear . . .'

'It's OK, I'll get the tube. Or the bus. Or something.'

'But, Jake—'

'I'm going.'

'No, you're not. I'll get you a duvet.'

Click to see previous comments

LizzieK Poppy was going to get pregnant? AWESOME.

ToniF Boring! Why can't scriptwriters think of different plots for women? Why is it always about babies?

LizzieK I reckon Poppy would've made a lovely mum.

ToniF And then months and months of who's the father? Like that's never been done before. Let's face it, *Market Square* had run out of ideas. Jake's dad did them a favour.

BobbyBroadbent Kirsty – if you're reading this – could we just talk?

Robster What's with the fade to black, mate? No action scenes with Kirsty Connor? Come on!!!

JakeBenn Just want to make it clear, nothing happened with Kirsty, OK? Nothing.

Click to load more comments

EPISODE 9

*The Benn family's kitchen/living room. Neil, Maria
and Jake are sitting at the table, newspapers spread out
in front of them. Adam is sitting on the sofa, watching*
Thomas the Tank Engine.

'All the papers, Jake. All of them! Front page of the
Mirror. Top story on the *Mail Online*'s Sidebar of Shame.'
'Neil, don't shout. It won't do any good.'
'How could you be so stupid? No one will want to
employ you. And they'll can Riley for sure.'

Jake looks up.

'Riley? Did you hear something?'
'No, but it can only be a matter of days. Did you see the

Sun? "We Know Where Riley's Been Hiding – in Kirsty's Bedroom!"'

'Well, at least I'm *in* the news. That's what they want, after all.'

'Who? Who wants to see a sixteen-year-old kid vomiting on the steps of his girlfriend's flat at 6 a.m.? Maria, why did you let him go?'

'I thought he was at a friend's house, Neil! Between work and Adam and commuting, I can hardly think straight.'

'Jake's way too young to be running round with a girl-friend of, what? Twenty-one? Twenty-three?'

'Is she your girlfriend, Jake? Kirsty? Isn't she a bit old for you?'

'No, she's not my girlfriend!'

'You could have told me where you were. Just a text home.'

'This flat isn't home. And she's just a colleague. An ex-colleague, as it turns out. And I wasn't planning to stay, it just worked out that way.'

'Look, Jake, you're old enough that I shouldn't have to lecture you about the birds and the bees. But this is not just about getting your leg over—'

'Neil, please!'

'I'm sorry, Maria, but I've got to be frank here. He's a normal young man and Kirsty's a lovely girl, stands to reason they'd find each other attractive.'

'Dad! Shut up!'

'I'm just saying. Paparazzi. Early mornings. It's very basic. Think before you shag.'

'Dad—'

'Think: is there going to be a snapper on the doorstep?'

'Dad—'

'And if you're shagging a soap star – sorry, Maria, *making love* to a soap star – then the answer is yes. Yes, there will be someone taking your picture as you barf up your breakfast. Yes, the *Mail* and the *Sun* will buy those pictures. Yes, your agent will call first thing the next day, absolutely horrified. And yes, you've probably ruined your chances of getting that Prince Jasper job, let alone going back to *Market Square*.'

'Well, that's rubbish actually. Because you know who they're considering for Riley? Bobby Broadbent.'

'Bobby who?'

'He's Kirsty's ex. He's off *The Real Cab Drivers of Colchester*.'

'Kirsty's ex? A reality star?'

'But, Jake, if he's Kirsty's ex, how can he play Riley?'

Neil's googling Bobby Broadbent.

'This guy? They're considering this guy? He looks about thirty.'

'He's twenty-one. He's going on a diet.'

'Riley's a teenager!'

'I know that.'

'This is outrageous. It's unacceptable. I'm going down to the *Market Square* set to have a word with them myself.'

'Look, Dad, Mum, leave it out, OK? You don't know anything. You don't know how the business works, you don't know how to talk to agents, and you're not safe in charge of a pile of money ...'

'Jake, darling, that's not fair—'

'How is it not fair? Is it fair that all my money has gone? Is it fair that I'm sharing a room with Adam?'

Adam reacts to the raised voices by burying his head in his hands and screaming. Maria rushes to his side.

'Oh, Adam, darling, it's alright. It really is. Jake didn't mean it.'

'Mum, he didn't understand what I was saying.'

'You both know we mustn't shout in front of him. It's so upsetting.'

Adam's still making noises of distress, rocking backwards and forwards.

'*Thomas*. Will someone put *Thomas* on for him. Oh, Adam. It's OK, sweetheart.'

'There's no point, Maria. He's in his own world.'

'Except he's not, Dad, because then we could shout all we wanted and he wouldn't notice.'

'You can't reason with him, that's what I mean. And you can't comfort him. And it's lucky your mother has the patience of a saint, because I bloody well haven't.'

'Neil—'

Adam's cries get louder.

'You've got everything, Jake. He's got nothing. And now you're throwing it all away.'

'That's complete crap.'

'I'm going down there to sort it out with Marcus. But you'd better shape up, son. No more scandals.'

'You can't go down there!'

'I can do whatever I think's best for my family. But right now, I'm going to the pub.'

Exit Neil.

Maria is trying to calm Adam, without touching him.
Jake's still sitting at the table.

'Mum, Kirsty's not my girlfriend. I just ... I had too much to drink. I stayed over. I did text you.'

'Jake, love, you can see I haven't got time for this now.'

'You never have time for me.'

'That's just not true.'

'It is though.'

*Adam's movements are getting bigger, his arms
flailing, his howls louder. He picks up a Thomas train
and throws it at the wall.*

'Adam! No! That's very naughty.'
'Mum, I can't stand this either. I'm going. I'll probably
stay at Orson's tonight.'

*Maria's trying to stop Adam from throwing more
trains. She doesn't hear Jake.*

'Bye then. Bye, Mum.'

Click to see previous comments

TheRealNoahBlaskett Hey, Dylan, just want to
congratulate you on the way you acted the autistic kid in
that episode. Really amazing work. Good job!
DestinyRock OMG, now Noah Blaskett is
commenting on the show! Thanks! Could you possibly
tweet a link to the episode?
Tammi♥Jake That Destiny girl is really annoying and
pushy. Who is she? Hope you're not too friendly with
her, Jake! Don't forget your true fans! We never believed
all the lies about Kirsty. She's way too old and ugly for
you. ♥
BobbyBroadbent Don't insult Kirsty. She's beautiful.

JuliefromGrimsby So, are you still seeing Kirsty, Jake? Because I thought, the way she behaved that last episode of *Market Square*, that might be because she's actually in love with you.

JakeBenn No, absolutely not.

Tammi♥Jake Yay!

Click to load more comments

PART 2

There is, sir, an eyrie of children, little eyases,
that cry out on the top of question and are most
tyrannically clapped for 't. These are now the fashion,
and so berattle the common stages – so they call them –
that many wearing rapiers are afraid of goose
quills and dare scarce come thither.

Hamlet, Act 2, scene 2.

PART 2

EPISODE 10

Orson's bedroom in west London. Orson is sitting at his desk, headphones on, looking at his laptop. Jake is lying on a futon. He doesn't look comfortable. The camera zooms in on Jake, who is learning his lines for the Prince Jasper callback.

Jake adopts a slightly foreign accent.

'I have trained as a swordsman with the finest blades in my father's kingdom. I have jousted and wrestled and lifted weights. I might look young, but I am strong and healthy. But this – I have never been treated like this. A prince of the Dark Isle, set to shovelling latrines.'

Pause.

'Latreens? Latrynes?'

Jake looks at his phone.

'OK. Set to shovelling latrines. The stench, the filth, the harsh treatment. I swear revenge!'

Jake takes a breath. Back to his normal voice.

'That's not bad actually. I've got all that. Just two pages to go. I'm normally good at learning lines, but it's harder this time.

'Going to be honest, it's not so comfortable staying at Orson's. This thing is a futon. They have them in Japan. I think their bones must be lighter than ours. Orson's mum, Alice – one of his mums – bought it so he could have friends to stay whenever he wanted. I guess it worked better when the friends were six.

'Now, I can feel the floor in every vertebra.

'Orson is my best friend, although we haven't got all that much in common. It's not been easy to find friends at school, to be honest. They tend to divide into three groups. There's the ones who are really keen to be my mate because they think I'll introduce them to celebrities. I try and avoid them. They're easy to spot because they'll start asking about the *Market Square* cast about five minutes into any conversation. What's Kirsty Connor like in real life? Is it true that Logan Winters drinks too much? Do you think of Angela Rose as your real mum?

'Then there are the ones who actively dislike me because I'm supposedly big-headed and false and full-of-myself and whatever. Destiny Rock, she's in my drama class and she's one of the worst. It's as though she's personally offended because I have a career, while she's just the biggest swot in the school.

'But Orson and Gilbert and Arthur, they're my mates because none of them give a toss about whether I'm famous or not. Orson is only meant to watch television for two hours a week. His mums think it inhibits creativity. Arthur likes French films and avant-garde art and has only heard of *Market Square* because of me. And Gilbert only moved to the UK from Brazil last year and hasn't got familiar with British popular culture yet.

'I'm crashing at Orson's again tonight. Third night in a row. I just couldn't face going back to the flat after that bust-up.

'I couldn't breathe in that place.

'I can't deal with it. I can't even think about Mum and Dad and the money and all that. It's too huge. I'm too angry. I need to be somewhere else. Home doesn't feel like home.

'The whole thing with Kirsty is so embarrassing. I drank too much. Woke up in the morning and had to rush off to get home and changed for school. I got out of the front door and just felt like death. And then I puked up the pizza all over her doorstep.

'Seriously, nothing else happened. But I'm not saying anything because, you know, it doesn't hurt if people think something is going on.

'I mean, Kirsty Connor. In my dreams.

'I probably should explain it properly to Mum. But I can't stand to see the look on her face when she hears that there's still nothing from *Market Square*. I've had no new auditions. And the callback for Prince Jasper has been put back a month because the director wants to be there and he's tied up with a gender-swap *Little Red Riding Hood*.

'I mean, not literally, but he's too busy for auditions. I'll hang on another month.

'Orson wouldn't care if I stayed forever, because I'm like one of the family. His mums like me, and his little sisters like me, and the food is good and I fit right in. Orson's even got his own bathroom, so I've stashed a toothbrush and some Lynx body spray here, and his mums don't seem to notice that I put my stuff into the wash.

'I suppose I'll have to go home at some point to pick up some more clothes, but maybe I can do it when my parents are out. Sometimes they take Adam out to the park or whatever. It's always awkward, but they think it's good for him.

'I'm really doing them a favour by staying away. One less mouth to feed and all that.

'But the futon's so sodding uncomfortable. Maybe I'll try Arthur's place tomorrow.

'OK, what's the next bit? The princess says, "Revenge for my father?" And I say . . . '

Jake puts on his Prince Jasper voice again.

'If he were not your father then I would order him executed, strung up by his neck like a puppet on a string. But I cannot. Because that would hurt you, and your sweetness is worth so much more than his harshness. Can't you see that? Can't you see that your much beloved father is evil?'

Click to see previous comments

Susie, Oxford That Prince Jasper film sounds terrible.

Tammi♥Jake I don't know why they make you audition! Don't they know how talented you are? Me and the rest of the Riley fans, we'll all come and see the film!!!!

Caring I've always found a futon very good for my back. I don't know what you're complaining about.

LizzieK Isn't that Dylan? Why are you calling him Orson? Is he taking more than one part? #confused

OrsonSwell There is no way on earth that you could get me to be in this crap, and I have not given permission for Dylan Johnson to 'act' being me.

Click to load more comments

EPISODE 11

Jake is in the school library with three friends, Gilbert, Arthur and Orson.

'Guys, I appreciate this. Gil, here's my maths homework ... Arthur, can you do the French, obviously. And the science? Orson ... geography, maybe? It's my worst subject so they don't expect much. I've done English and drama. I've really got to work on the pages for the callback for this film.'

'What's the film, Jake?'

'It's one of those epic fantasy things. A young prince. He's put in charge of an army, but it all goes tits up, and he's captured by a weird hermit who makes him work like a slave, then he falls in love with the guy's daughter. That's all I know.'

'Do you get any action?'

Orson kisses the back of his hand, with much tongue-waggling.

'Full frontal sex scenes? A chance to dirty up the child star image?'

'I don't know. Maybe. First I have to get the part, then they talk details with my agent.'

'And do you get to go away?'

'Three months in Croatia. Sun, sand and real work.'

'You get all the luck. And you expect us to do your homework.'

'Like I say, really appreciated.'

'Don't worry, mate. An honour to do your geography for you. Just remember us when you pick up your Oscar.'

Jake's friends take his books and get to work. Destiny, another Year 11 student, emerges from behind a bookshelf. She looks disapproving.

'Cheating again?'

'Well, if it isn't Hermione Granger.'

'Shut up, Orson, I was talking to Jake.'

'Well he's not interested in talking to you.'

'Oh, he's too grand to speak for himself now, is he? Needs you to protect him?'

Destiny scans the library.

'Can't see many fangirls myself, but maybe I'm wrong. Maybe you need to protect Jake against the hordes of invisible stalkers that chase him through the streets of London.'

Jake is exasperated.

'Shut up, Destiny.'

'Oh, he knows my name! I'm going to die of joy.'

'Yeah, right, OK. Very funny.'

'Cheating is not funny.'

'I'm not cheating. If I were cheating I wouldn't ask Orson to do my geography.'

'I'm alright at geography!'

'Orson, you think Sydney is the capital of Australia.'

'Sydney *is* the capital of Australia!'

'Destiny, leave us alone, OK? It's none of your business. I've got a bit of a domestic crisis. It's not the capital, Orson. Google it.'

'A crisis? Has your manicurist taken a day off? Maybe you've got a spot on your nose?'

'Like you *haven't*, crater face?'

Jake and Destiny speak at the same time.

'Shut *up*, Orson.'

'Oh, come on, Destiny, the guys are just helping me get up to date. Standard practice.'

Destiny's not responding to Jake's winning smile.

'They're doing your homework for you.'

'They don't mind, do you, guys? Orson likes geography. He's crazy about tectonic plates.'

'I mind. It's breaking the rules. It's not fair.'

'What rules? The school knows that I need help catching up sometimes. That's what happens when you have a life outside school. Not that you'd know that.'

'You haven't been away working for ages though. You ought to be taking responsibility for your own homework.'

'What is your problem, Destiny? Why can't you mind your own business?'

'It's just not fair, that's all. You ought to do your own stuff.'

'What's it to you?'

'Nothing. I mean, I just care in an abstract way. I care about equality and honesty and I'm anti-cheating. Getting Orson to do your geography is a slippery slope.'

'A slippery slope to where?'

'To being some prat of a celebrity who can't even peel his own grapes. One day it'll be this lot, the next you'll be the sort of tosser who has an entourage.'

Arthur, Gilbert and Orson whistle derisively.

'Get that, an entourage.'
'Someone's jealous . . . '
'She *likes* you. Too bad, Destiny, he's with Kirsty Connor.'

Destiny and Jake speak at the same time again.

'Shut *up*, Orson.'

Click to see previous comments

Tammi♥Jake That Destiny girl again! She's not even pretty! She's nasty to you! Why are you friends with her now?

DestinyRock Back off with your personal comments, OK?

Tammi♥Jake And you've got a stupid name.

DestinyRock 1) I moderate these comments. Consider yourself warned. 2) I have an awesome name. Funnily enough, I'm going to talk about it in the next episode. Which is all about me. Suck it up, sister.

Click to load more comments

EPISODE 12

Destiny's bedroom is small and tidy. She has a revision timetable pinned to the wall. She also has a bookcase packed with books, and a small desk. She's sitting, cross-legged on her bed.

'We decided it was time for me to have my say, as maybe I came across a little bit bossy in the last episode.

'My name is Destiny Rock. And I am bossy. I admit it. It's my main flaw. I don't care. I'm not here to win a popularity contest.

'One day I want to be a film director, and that's a job for a bossy person. My mum says I should dream on, that's not going to happen, you need money for that. But I always say, there's no point being called Destiny unless you have a destination in mind.

'When I was eleven, I had a destination in mind: the posh school down the road. You don't get many people who look like me in there; it's all white and Asian kids. It was me who found out that they had scholarships. It was me who passed the exams to get in. And it's me who's worked hard to stay there as well.

'Jake Benn drove me mad. It wasn't because I fancied him. That's just what his friends said to shut me up. That's how girls get silenced at our school. Ha ha, she fancies him, don't listen to her, she's in love.

'I have no interest in stupid teenage romances. Just want to make that clear, OK?

'Jake Benn annoyed me because he didn't take school very seriously, and he was hardly ever there anyway. He seemed to have everything just fall into his lap. He was in the world that I wanted to be in, although he was in front of the camera not behind it. I admit it, I was jealous, but he didn't do himself any favours. He was a bit exclusive about it. You could tell he thought we were all just kids and he was like some sort of grown-up.

'I just didn't see what he was being so superior about. I'd watched *Market Square*. I mean, I know a lot of people loved it, but it wasn't all that. It wasn't even particularly representative of London. Those Khans, they were the only people of colour in the whole programme.

'In my opinion it wasn't a bad thing that it got cancelled.

'Just saying.

'I want to pass my exams and go to Film School. Ideally in New York. Failing that, I'm going to study Theatre at university here. I'll find the money somehow. I'll find a way.

'Being a director is everything. There's the writer, sure, but there's only so much they can do. Even with someone like Shakespeare – the director decides how to stage the play. What the characters look like. How they sound. What the words mean. Even which words to use and which to leave out.

'And Jake, he'd be great, because you can see he's got a good range. That annoyed me too. He was genuinely a good actor, but he wouldn't take part in school productions because ... well, I thought it was because he felt that he was too good for us.

'I didn't know him very well at that point.

'I didn't realise what was going on in his life.'

EPISODE 13

Orson's kitchen is full of family life – children's artwork on the fridge, plastic plates and cups. Orson's eating a large breakfast and watching his laptop.

Enter Kate, one of Orson's mothers. She's got a baby on her hip and she's clearly not happy.

'Orson, Jake's in the bathroom. I told you I have to be out early today.'

Orson doesn't hear her. He's too busy watching his screen. Kate removes his headphones. Violent sounds fill the kitchen. Orson reluctantly turns his phone off.

'Oy, Mum! Give them back. That was just the most exciting bit. Seriously, blood everywhere!'

'You've had your screen time for the week. And you know we hate you watching that programme. So much gratuitous sex and violence.'

'That's what makes it so good. I can't believe you don't understand that.'

'Orson! Anyway, you've got to get Jake out of the bathroom. I told you I've got an early start.'

'He won't be long. I'm eating.'

Orson tries to help himself to more cereal but the packet is empty.

'Mum? Can you get more Cheerios?'

'Is that the last of the Cheerios? What are the twins going to have for their breakfast? Orson, I can't keep up with feeding two teenage boys. You and Jake were eating bowls of cereal at midnight last night. It's like I'm running Jurassic Park.'

'Bit of an overstatement, Mum.'

'Look, we love Jake, you know we do, but he's been here for two weeks now. I'm beginning to wonder if he's ever going to leave. What's the story, Orson?'

'Aw, come on, he's my mate. I don't know what's going on. He just needs somewhere to stay, for a bit. I don't know how long. He might go to Croatia.'

'Croatia?'

'If he gets this film role.'

'What's wrong with his own home?'

'Mum! That's a bit personal.'

'You mean you don't even know why he's staying?'

'It's just that he fancied a change of scene.'

'Well look, tonight is Mum's birthday. We're all going to Pizza Express. That's you, Leo, Finn and Maddy. Not Jake. It's family only.'

'Oh, that's OK. Jake'll be fine here on his own. He doesn't even like pizza anymore.'

'Sweetie, Jake needs to sort out whatever's wrong with his own family situation. I had his mum on the phone the other day. She was absolutely distraught.'

Neither of them notice Jake in the doorway, dressed in school uniform.

'Jeez, Mum, stop making it all into such a drama.'

'I'm not. I'm just concerned. Two weeks, Orson.'

'His dad did a bit of a nuclear explosion about Kirsty Connor. I don't know why, because you couldn't get a fitter girlfriend.'

'That's enough objectifying women.'

'God, Mum . . . '

Jake backs away. A door slams.

'What was that? Why was the door open?'

'I dunno.'

'Well, maybe Jake's out of the shower now. I'll go and have a look.'

'Mum, you wouldn't throw him out, would you? Mum?'

'Of course not. But we're going to have to have a proper chat. And maybe he can find somewhere else for tomorrow.'

'You're so mean.'

'Jake needs to face up to his problems, whatever they are.'

Orson reaches for his headphones.

'You're meaner than Cersei Lannister.'

'Luckily for you, son, I have no idea who she is.'

Click to see previous comments

OrsonSwell So you were spying on us for that whole conversation? Nice. Or did you just make it up?

JakeBenn I'm just trying to tell the story, Orson.

OrsonSwell You don't like it when photographers take your picture, but it's fine to completely make up a conversation between me and my mum? Invade our privacy? Make my mum look mean?

JakeBenn I didn't mean to do that.

74

OrsonSwell Get lost, loser.

DestinyRock No abuse, Orson, or I'll have to censor you.

OrsonSwell COMMENT REMOVED BY MODERATOR.

MarketSquareFan I think we're losing sight of the real issue here. Can you get a show insider to tell us about Amina's wedding? And all the other hanging storylines? I'm having trouble sleeping at night.

LizzieK Having Kirsty Connor play the mum of a kid drooling about Kirsty Connor – that's just weird.

DestinyRock We thought it was a bold casting decision. Sort of post-modern.

OrsonSwell Do you even know what post-modern means, Destiny?

DestinyRock Of course. Post-modern theatre highlights the fallibility of definite truth, encouraging the audience to reach their own understanding. It asks questions rather than supplying answers.

OrsonSwell Anyone can cut and paste from Wikipedia.

DestinyRock As Richard Foreman said, 'No work of art is absolutely truthful about life but is a strategic manoeuvre performed on a coagulated consciousness.'

OrsonSwell *What?????*

DestinyRock Or, to quote Picasso (he's an artist, Orson, look him up): 'Art is a lie that tells the truth.'

OrsonSwell So you admit that whole scene was a total lie? (And I know who Picasso is, thank you, Destiny.)

DestinyRock *eyeroll*

LizzieK You know who you two remind me of? Ron and Hermione!

Click to load more comments

EPISODE 14

Jake's in the park near school, sitting on a swing, talking into his phone. On a split screen we see the people he's talking to.

'Kirsty? I've been trying to call you for ages. Have you been blocking me? Did you get my messages?'

'Don't leave messages, Jake. It's not a good idea.'

'I know mobile phones get hacked. I know. But they're meant to have stopped doing that now . . . I'm sorry, Kirsty.'

'I was totally embarrassed by those stories.'

'I didn't know there would be a photographer. I should've realised.'

'So you didn't do it on purpose, to get attention?'

'I'm not desperate. I don't want that sort of attention. Jesus, Kirsty!'

'Just thought you might be trying to get the eye of the *Market Square* producers. As that's how they seem to be doing their casting right now.'

'Look, I'm just not ... things aren't great at the moment, and I need somewhere to stay. Obviously not at yours, I know. I understand that. I just thought you might know someone, someone in the business. Someone who'd understand. Just until I can—'

'You're sixteen, Jake. You ought to be at home with your parents.'

'Yes, I'm only sixteen. You don't need to rub it in. But I don't feel sixteen. I feel at least as old as you.'

'Charming.'

'OK, I'm not saying you're old. You're only twenty-one. C'mon, Kirsty. I'm sorry, OK? Did they ... have they said anything about it on the Square? Like Marcus, did he say anything?'

'I told him it was a fuss about nothing.'

'OK, so he didn't seem too angry? You don't think it was a deal-breaker?'

'You should talk to your agent.'

'Yes, obviously. OK ... well ... sorry. I'm really sorry. Bye, Kirsty.'

Jake ends the call, thinks for a few moments, then finds another number. He takes a deep breath.

'Can I speak to Zoe Millard, please? It's Jake. Jake

Benn. Yes. Yes, that's me. I'm fine. Really, yes, I am. It was gastric flu. Yeah, much better now.'

There's a pause. Jake's showing the stress.

'Zoe? Hey, it's Jake. How are you? Everything good, I hope?'

'Jake! How are you? I've been trying to get hold of you. How are you? Everything alright?'

'Me? No, I'm fine. I'm really sorry about the pictures – just a stomach upset, bit unfortunate.'

'So you and Kirsty? Are you together?'

'No! Zoe, she's like five years older than me.'

'You know Marcus called me the day those pictures were published?'

'Really? Marcus rang you about me? What did he say? He didn't—'

'He wanted to know what you were playing at. He didn't say anything about the part.'

'Nothing?'

'He said they're still deciding what to do.'

'How long do they need?'

'The Elliott family aren't part of the biggest storylines at the moment. There's all this stuff around the Khans. Some wedding . . . extremism . . .'

'Yeah, but the Elliotts are still in it.'

'He said something about deciding soon because Amina's wedding is coming up and then the Elliotts are going to move centre stage.'

'Really? And Riley?'

'Well, he's part of the family. Be patient, Jake.'

'I am. It's just hard, not knowing. I'm learning the stuff for Prince Jasper. I really want that part. It's just—'

'You going to be alright for the fourth? That's when they want to see you.'

'Yes. Dylan's still in it too. He's been in touch.'

'I'm backing you to get this one, Jake. Fingers crossed.'

'Thanks, Zoe. Bye.'

Jake ends the call, puffs out his cheeks, exhales. The next call is the hardest.

'Mum? It's me.'

'Jake? Jake, are you going to come home tonight? I haven't seen you all week.'

'I'm fine, Mum. I'm staying with friends.'

'You can't stay with friends for ever! Orson's mum said you'd been there for weeks.'

'It's easier. My friends live nearer school. I can't commute from Essex to west London every day. It's too much.'

'Sweetheart, come home. This is ridiculous.'

'No. No, I can't. No.'

'But why not?'

'Because of everything, Mum. Because of the money and the house, and the whole Kirsty thing. I feel like it's all my fault, because I'm not Riley anymore.'

'It's not your fault. Don't think that. It's hard times for all of us. We need to stick together as a family.'

'It's just, Dad's getting so stressed, and I seem to make it worse. And I can't get ready for this audition and learn the pages if he's all uptight. And he is, Mum, I haven't seen him this bad for ages, since ... you know, since he lost his job. That flat's too small to hide it even if he could.'

'He doesn't mean it, darling, he really doesn't. He loves all of us so much.'

'Look, I've got the Prince Jasper callback coming up. That's really positive. And if I get it, then it's three months in Croatia, and I can give you some money, and—'

'What about your GCSEs? What about your mocks?'

'I don't care about GCSEs. Exams are less important than my career right now.'

'I don't know about that ...'

'Mum, I can make these decisions for myself. I know more about acting than you do.'

'Jake, we miss you. Don't push us away. Come home, darling.'

'Don't cry, Mum. Please don't.'

Maria's struggling to hold back the tears.

'Give my love to Adam.'
'He loves you, Jake.'
'Oh, OK. In his own way, yeah, right, Mum.'

'Tomorrow, Jake? Come home Friday? For the weekend?'

'No. It's just too much. Sorry. I mean, I'm not sorry. Dad should be sorry.'

'Please, Jake?'

'Give me time, OK? Give me time.'

Jake makes one more call.

'Hey, Gil. Are you around tonight? I was just wondering, could I crash at your place tonight? I'm just ... I'd really appreciate it.'

Click to see previous comments

ConcernedMum Your poor mum. I'd be worried sick if my son started staying with friends all the time.

Caring Bit selfish of you, Jake.

MarketSquareFan So the storyline around the Khan family – that was about to come to a head? Please tell us what you know. I think the BBC should have the decency to publish all the scripts that had been written beyond the point where they pulled the plug.

Soaphead Good luck with that! The BBC never listens to its loyal viewers. I've complained so often – most recently about Fiona Bruce's eyebrows – and they never do a thing.

LizzieK What's wrong with Fiona Bruce's eyebrows?

Soaphead Crooked. Patronising. Right-wing.

DramaticDee At least she's a woman! By choosing someone who is not a symbol of the patriarchy to front *News at Ten*, at least the BBC is paying lip service to the questions that we all have to ask about fairness, democracy and bias. But Fiona Bruce (accomplished though she is) is far from an ideal choice. Even when a female PoC reads the news, there is still an inherent middle-class ownership of current affairs, one that is rarely challenged. I'd like to see a really great list of alternative presenters on *News at Ten*, people with all sorts of accents and faces, sexualities and genders, including trans and gender-fluid presenters. How about getting Malala to read the news? Wouldn't that be amazing?

Click to load more comments

EPISODE 15

Gil's house. Jake's sitting on the bottom bunk in the room of a much smaller child. His bed is covered with soft toys. Gil's six-year-old brother is asleep on the top bunk.

'OK, this is awkward.

'Bit embarrassing, really.

'I mean, I'm friends with Gil and everything, and I just didn't know he was having people over tonight. I didn't think. He didn't say.

'I always forget that he has all these out of school friends who are Brazilian like him, and when they get together they like to speak Portuguese. I mean, I like Gil and everything, but I don't know him that well. He arrived at school when I was working away, and then

Orson and Arthur made friends with him, and we've never really, you know, assessed our friendship.

'Still, it was nice of him to say I could stay, and it's better than, well . . . I probably could have found someone else to stay with. Definitely. I hadn't even begun . . . Gil was the first one I rang. It's just a bit boring, asking lots of people.

'There's Dylan, I suppose, but he's not . . . he's an acting friend. I don't want to have everyone knowing my business. I could ask Dylan, his parents know me, but . . . every time I ring someone and ask, it feels a bit more rubbish. A bit more desperate.

'I never really had friends over at home. Adam gets unsettled when there are strangers in the house. It's never worth unsettling Adam. He gets noisy, throws things. I mean, it's sad to see him like that. No one wants it.

'Apparently he was normal when he was little. Just like any kid. Talking and everything. Beginning to talk, anyway. Actual words.

'Then I was born, and it was as though he stopped. He went backwards. He lost words. He didn't learn any new ones. He stopped smiling.

'It wasn't connected with me being born. That's what they always say, anyway. It was just a coincidence of timing. Apparently it happens quite often to kids around his age.

'By the time I was talking, he'd stopped altogether.

I wanted him to talk to me so much. I swear, I tried everything. My earliest memory is of talking and talking to Adam, asking him questions, giving him toys, showing him pictures I'd drawn.

'And he never said a word.

'Mum reckons that's why I'm a performer, because I tried so hard with Adam. I wanted to entertain him. As soon as I was old enough I begged her to take me to classes in drama, music, dance.

'I loved it. I still love it. I act, people react. I need that. It's basic.

'But also, acting was an escape. A way to stay out of the house, because I never really accepted that all my effort was pointless. Adam wasn't going to react in the way I wanted him to. He was never going to start laughing or talking.

'He'd never be normal.

'And I didn't feel normal either. I felt like I was acting all the time. I was this nice, loving, helpful brother. But it was all a performance. It was all fake.

'Nonna understood. She used to talk about it sometimes when we were on the way to an audition. "So much hard work for your parents," she'd say. "And you trying to help all the time, Jake. You shouldn't have to feel like that. You're old before your time."

'I told her that I was fine. I loved acting. I loved being treated like an adult. I loved being able to help my parents with some money, see them smile, see them relax for once.

'But then Nonna died and Riley disappeared and I couldn't do that anymore.

'I just don't know where my life is going. Who I am anymore. I've been Riley for so long, for one thing. And if I can't be Riley then I'm still an actor.

'But what if I never get another acting job? Who am I then?

'I don't really know who I am anymore.

'That's why I can't go home.'

Click to see previous comments

JakeBenn I just want to say thank you for all the nice comments I've had here. I'm really overwhelmed. You're very kind. It makes me feel like making this series is 100% worthwhile.

Caring i found it very moving. Thanks for sharing, Jake.

OrsonSwell You've turned into a complete luvvie, you know that? Makes me want to vomit.

DestinyRock Why can't you just be nice, Orson? Anyway, heads up, the next episode is meant to be on the set of *Market Square*. We had to improvise with Dylan's garden furniture. And Angie and Kirsty are playing themselves, playing the Elliotts. Obviously.

Click to load more comments

EPISODE 16

A trestle table with some bowls of fruit. Kirsty Connor and Angela Rose are selling fruit and vegetables. Angela is calling out to passers-by, while Kirsty serves customers. The extras, shopping in the market, are played by Destiny, Arthur and Gil.

'Banana, banana! Lovely fresh strawberries!'
'Two for a pound. Want some, love? Here you go.'
'Banana, banana!'
'I've got a lovely pair of melons!'

Someone calls 'Cut!' The customers disperse, some sitting down. Kirsty's exasperated.

'Who writes this stuff? I've got a lovely pair of melons? That's borderline offensive.'

'Should've guessed when they gave us a fruit stall, darling. Why are we waiting around now? What's going on?'

'We've lost Logan. Got to find him.'

'He'll be in the Green Room. Dozy boy. If he really was my son, I'd give him what for.'

'Like to see that, Angie. Maybe you shouldn't take him out clubbing 'til the early hours?'

'Ah, Kirsty, you should come with us sometime. You've got to let your hair down more often. Better than staying in and eating pizza with a sixteen-year-old boy.'

'I wondered when that'd come up, *Mum*.'

'I'm not stupid enough to think that anything happened between you and Jake, but I do think that you should've known better than to ply him with alcohol.'

'Oh, c'mon, Angie. He's a big boy. It was only a couple of glasses of wine!'

They haven't noticed, but Jake is approaching them through the market.

'It's true, it was only a bit of wine.'

'Jake?'

'Jake?'

Everyone on set is stunned. Someone off camera calls 'Go and get Marcus!'

'What are you doing here, darling? Come here, and give your old mum a hug. Look at you! Looking a bit better than you did in those pictures in the *Mail*, eh?'

'Hi, Ange, it's good to see you. I've really missed everyone.'

'So you thought you'd come back for a visit? It's just that we're in the middle of everything right now, darling. Just waiting for Logan. Oh, here he is.'

Enter Logan.

'Riley! Bruv!'

'Hey, Logan.'

'They let you out of your bedroom at last? Nice one! Must've missed that in the script . . . I'm a bit under the weather.'

'No, not really, I just wanted to come and talk to Marcus myself.'

Enter Marcus.

'Jake. Darling. Sweetheart. What the frig are you doing here?'

'Marcus. Umm. Hi.'

'Lovely though it is to see you, this is not the time or the place, sweetie. Why don't you . . . Claire! Why doesn't Claire take you to get a lemonade in the canteen, and then she can call you a cab home?'

'It's just, I thought if I turned up, I could just have a quick word, Marcus. It's been a long time.'

'How did you get in? Oh, I see, you still have your pass. Claire! Claire! Where is she?'

'Aw, go on, Marcus. Have a chat with Jake. He's our little brother, innit? Been on the show a long time.'

Marcus gives Logan a long, disapproving glare.

'Lot of the viewers miss him.'

'Well, OK, then. At least then you can get on with this scene. This crucial scene. Don't be late again, Logan. I can't afford to carry baggage on this show, darling, even including you.'

'Sorry, slept through my alarm.'

'Come along then, Jake.'

Jake follows Marcus to a side room, just off the set. In the background the action starts again, with Angela shouting about bananas, and Kirsty and Logan arguing.

'So, Jake. Long time no see.'

'Yeah, well, that's it really. That's why I'm here. I thought, if I came to see you, showed you that I've really grown up a lot over the last year—'

'Is that what the stunt at Kirsty's flat was all about? Classy.'

'No, that was an accident. But I'm a lot taller now, and my teeth are completely straight and I've been working on my fitness. I mean, I think I look older. I could cope with more adult storylines.'

'The problem is that the viewers still see you as that cherubic kid they fell in love with. No amount of muscle's going to change that. Will they buy you as a grown-up Riley, getting involved in all sorts? That's what I've been pondering.'

'I would've thought so. I mean, people do grow up.'

'Have you got the range, Jake? Can you do more than cute?'

'I can, I'm sure I can. I mean, already, Riley got in with that gang, and there was the thing with the knife.'

'Truth is, I'm not sure I'd be doing you a favour if I kept you on. You're what, sixteen? You don't want to be typecast at sixteen. You need to get a training, widen your experience. Pass a few exams.'

'I don't care about exams. Or a training. I just want to work as an actor.'

'You should care. Do you know how many actors are employed in the business on anything like a regular basis? A tiny percentage. Getting a job like you've had, a regular job, appearing on TV every week, that's like finding gold in your garden pond.'

'I know.'

'You do? Because I got the impression that your agent was beginning to take it for granted, trying to renegotiate your contract.'

'It might have been my dad putting pressure on her. Look, Marcus, he might turn up. My dad. He says he's going to come and talk to you, and I don't want you to think—'

'Wouldn't be the first time.'

'I know, but—'

'I haven't got time for interfering parents, Jake. Sad, but true. Someone should get him under control.'

'I know. Believe me, I'm trying.'

'Thing is, no star is bigger than the show and you can tell your dad that from me. Not even someone like Logan, let alone a kid like you. I'm considering what I do with Riley, and it might be you, or it might be someone else. That's my decision. Pulling stunts like this – it won't work.'

'It's not a stunt.'

'Oh really?'

'It's not a stunt. I just wanted to cut out all the agents and parents and stuff. I love playing Riley and I'd like to come back. Please. That's all.'

'I'm sorry, kid. I can't make any promises. You hate me now, but you might be thanking me one day.'

'Why?'

'You might not want to be a soap star forever. You might not like being labelled. A lot of people sneer at what we do here. They think it's low culture. Entertainment for the masses.'

'But I don't think that.'

'They don't realise that soaps are the very essence of drama.'

'Yes. I mean, I agree.'

'We change people's lives. We empower them by showing them that their everyday dramas matter, that they are interesting, that they are important. We make everyday life into something special and important. That's not a small thing, Jake.'

'I know, that's why I'm—'

'When else do you see working-class lives on television? When people are sneering at them in documentaries and reality shows. Treating them like animals in the zoo. We give them dignity. We put them centre stage!'

'I agree, that's why I'm here. My life has gone a bit *Market Square*, and—'

The door opens and Claire, an assistant producer, comes in.

'Ah, Claire, there you are. Took your time. Can you take Jake to the canteen, get him milk and biscuits or whatever young people prefer nowadays? And then get him a cab home.'

'Sure. Come on, Jake.'

'Oh, and Claire. Make sure Jake gives you his security pass before he goes, please.'

Click to see previous comments

MarketSquareFan That Marcus, he's got a lot to answer for. Cutting great characters like Ruby Telford and Benny Moran. Introducing that whole stupid storyline about the market being bulldozed for a new tube line. No wonder people watch reality shows. No wonder the actors got fed up.

LizzieK Maybe he was doing Jake a favour. Look at those sad guys who've been in one show all their lives. That's not acting, it's stagnating.

BevfromBrighton I disagree. Spending your whole working life building up one character's story – that's the ultimate in acting, surely? The boundaries between actor and character become completely blurred. It must be a fascinating experience.

Tammi♥Jake It's only fascinating if Jake's in it.

Click to load more comments

EPISODE 17

Jake and Dylan, sitting side by side, waiting to be auditioned again.

'Look, Jake, no offence, mate, but are you OK? Really? Because you look a bit—'

'Mind your own business, Dylan.'

'A bit rough, to be honest. You going for some sort of Method approach? Simon Steinberg's a big believer in Method.'

Jake looks away.

'I can see that. I mean Prince Jasper has been roughing it for some time, hasn't he? Camped out in the forest with

96

the resistance fighters. Maybe I've missed a trick. Well
done, anyway, brave move.'

'Leave it out, Dylan.'

'No, I mean it. Look, best man wins and all that. We've
never really been rivals, have we? I mean, we've both had
good luck. We all win some and lose some.'

'Yeah, yeah, whatever.'

'Are you OK? You just seem a bit—'

'A bit what?'

'I don't know ... intense? Angry?'

Jake takes a deep breath.

'I'm fine, just tired.'

'I know, it's a lot to fit in, isn't it? GCSEs and all that.
My school are letting me just do eight subjects, but even
so.'

'I don't care about exams.'

'Nor do I, really, but I want to keep my options open.
Luckily GCSEs are easy, aren't they?'

'Yeah, right. Really easy.'

*A door bursts open, and Neil comes into the room,
arguing noisily with someone behind him. Jake's
completely horrified.*

'I need to see my son! I know parents aren't allowed
in, but ... OK, OK. It's an emergency, alright?'

'Dad!'

'Jake!'

'Go away. I've got an audition in about fifteen minutes.'

'And I'm your father! I've put so much into your career—'

'Dad, I just can't do this now. Go away.'

'You've got to come home. Your mum is so upset. Even Adam's noticed that you've gone. He's affected.'

'Don't try and guilt trip me. Adam hasn't got a clue whether I'm there or not.'

'He's been throwing his trains at the window.'

'That's nothing to do with me!'

'We're a family, Jake. We love each other.'

'How can Adam love anyone? He doesn't even speak.'

Dylan stands up.

'Look, I'm sorry to interrupt, but I'm about to go into an audition. And so is Jake. This isn't really helping either of us. Can't you talk afterwards?'

Neil opens his mouth to protest, and then closes it again.

'Dad, just go away. Please. Let me do this.'

'I'm coming into your audition.'

'Dad, you can't do that.'

'I want to be there to support you.'

'It's not going to help.'

'You can't dismiss me, Jake. You can't sack me. You can't make me redundant. I'm your dad for life, whether you like it or not.'

'You are, Dad, but you don't need to control everything I do!'

'You can't just walk out on us.'

'Dad, please.'

'I'm coming into that studio with you. I'll go and sort it out with them.'

Neil leaves the room, and Jake buries his head in his hands. Dylan is embarrassed, but attempts comfort.

'It's OK. You can sort it out later.'

'I ... yes, thanks.'

'It's nothing. Look, I'll go first. Give you a bit of time.'

'No, I'm OK. I can do it.'

Jake takes a breath.

'Prince Jasper ... he probably feels a bit like you do ...'

'Just leave it, OK? I appreciate your support and all that, but I need to concentrate on the sodding words now, OK? Just the words. I've worked so hard ... He's just ... Just the words.'

'OK. Stay calm.'
'OK.'

The casting assistant puts her head around the door.

'Jake? They're ready for you now.'

EPISODE 18

Jake stands all alone at one side of the room. He is watched by a panel of people – the casting director, the director and their assistants. He is waiting for them to stop talking.

Neil is sitting to one side, silently watching.

The casting director has a New York accent and an encouraging face.

'OK, Jake, let's go. You're a prince, fallen on hard times. You're in love. You're being treated as a slave by her father. All the emotions, please.'

Jake takes a sip of water. His hand is shaking. He stands up. He's forgotten his Prince Jasper voice.

101

'I have trained as a swordsman with the finest blades in my father's kingdom. I have jousted and wrestled and lifted weights. I might look young, but I am strong and healthy. Um. Sorry. Can I try that again?'

'OK, Jake. When you're ready.'

Jake remembers the accent, but not very well.

'I have trained as a swordsman with the finest swords in my father's . . . in my father's . . . '

'No worries, Jake. Do you need a script?'

'I don't . . . Yes. I'm sorry.'

'That's OK. Here you go.'

Jake raises his voice, attempts to become a young, strong prince.

'I have trained as a swordsman with the finest blades in my father's kingdom. I have jousted and wrestled and lifted weights. I might look young, but I am strong and healthy. But this – I have never been treated like this. A prince of the Dark Isle, set to shovelling latrines. The stench, the filth, the harsh treatment. I swear revenge.'

'Revenge against my father?'

'If he were not your father then I would order him executed, strung up by his neck like a puppet on a string. But I cannot. Because that would hurt you, and your sweetness is worth so much more than his evil.

I mean his harshness. Sorry. I skipped a line there. Sorry.'

'Jake, do you want to take a break? You seem . . . not yourself.'

'No, I'm . . . I'm . . . I'll keep going.'

'OK. Line.'

'Revenge against my father?'

'If he were not your father . . . your father . . . '

'Jake?'

'I'm sorry. I can't do it. Give Dylan the part.'

Neil stands up.

The casting director is sympathetic.

'You're having an off day. Look, go home. We can see you another day. We'll speak to your agent.'

'I can't . . . '

'It's OK.'

Neil loses it.

'It's not OK. He's doing it on purpose. He's trying to mess it up!'

'Dad, I'm not.'

'Mr Benn? I don't think this is helpful—'

'What do you think you're doing, Jake? Making some point just to spite me?'

'No, Dad. Please ... '

'Mr Benn, please ... '

'You know how much we need you to get this job.'

'Dad, I can't ... '

'No, I've had enough. Go running to your friends, for all I care. You're not welcome in my home anymore.'

A security guard suggests that Neil leaves the room. He's furious, but he obeys. Jake waits until he's gone.

'Look, I'm really sorry about that. My dad ... he suffers from stress. He goes a bit over the top. He didn't mean to.'

The casting director leans forward.

'Are you alright, Jake? Is there anyone we should call for you?'

'No, I'm fine. Please, just forget that, please.'

Exit Jake.

The casting director sighs, and looks at her colleagues.

'Stage parents, eh?'

PART 3

When sorrows come, they come not single spies.
But in battalions!

Hamlet, Act 4, scene 5.

EPISODE 19

Orson's house. Kate is sorting out washing. Orson and Jake are eating.

'Orson, you should ask Jake if he wants any more before you scrape out the dish.'

'What? Oh. Sorry, Jake.'

'No worries.'

'If you're still hungry, Jake, help yourself to some toast. Peanut butter in the cupboard. Or Nutella. You look half starved.'

'I'm fine. Honestly, I'm fine.'

Kate sits down at the table, looking Jake up and down.

'But you're not, are you? You're hungry, you don't look well, and you've got bags under your eyes.'

'Mum! Rude.'

'Have you been home at all, Jake? Your mum rang me today to ask if I'd seen you. She was so worried about you.'

'Mum, quit the interrogation.'

'Why don't I just ring her? She could come and get you.'

'Mum, Jake's perfectly welcome here. He's my friend. It's nothing to do with you where he stays.'

'I'm worried about you, Jake. Anyone would be. I've spoken to Arthur's mum, and Gil's too. It looks like you've been spending all your time going from house to house, futon to sofa bed, to mattress . . .'

'I'm fine. I'm not even going to stay over tonight. Just thought I'd come round to help Orson with his homework.'

'Your mum's been in touch with the school, you know. She's ringing every day to find out if you're turning up.'

'Well, I am. It's not like I've got anything better to do.'

'That's good. Have some fruit. Are you getting your five-a-day? Have an apple. Have an orange.'

'Thanks.'

'Look, I can run you home if you want. I know it's a bit of a way, now you've moved, but I can put the baby in the car seat, and she'll go to sleep.'

'No, really, I'm OK. I can get the tube. I'm fine.'

'I'd offer you a spare room, if we had one. Just while

you get over this ... whatever it is. Just to tide you over. But we don't have one, and I know how much your mum wants you home, and really, Jake, it's the best for everyone.'

'Sure, thanks. The pasta bake was awesome.'

'I'm sorry. Look, let me take you somewhere. To the station at least.'

'No, that's OK. I can manage.'

'I don't want you to feel unwelcome. We're worried about you.'

'Mum! You're totally embarrassing me. Jake stays in my room, it's fine.'

'I'm sorry, Orson, but you've got homework to do, and chores. You can't get all that done if Jake's staying every other night. And I can't imagine how you're coping with schoolwork, Jake, if you never go home. Where are all your books?'

'I don't ... it's fine. Thanks for supper. I'd better be off.'

'You will go home? It's much better to sort things out with your parents than feel like a cuckoo in the nest elsewhere.'

'I will. I'm going to.'

'Look, Mum, Jake got bad news today. It's not really the right day to throw him out on the street.'

'I'm not! I'm offering to drive him home. I'll come in with you if you want, Jake, try and get things sorted with your dad. What bad news?'

'His friend Dylan got that part. Prince Jasper. Three months filming in Croatia.'

'Oh dear. Oh, I am so sorry, Jake. But, you know, you win some, you lose some. It's inevitable, in the game you're in.'

'It's not a game.'

'No. No, of course not. Well, naturally it's disappointing.'

Jake stands up. He picks up the apple and the orange.

'I'd better go. Thanks again.'

Exit Jake.

The front door slams. Orson and his mum stare at each other.

'What the hell, Mum?'

'That didn't go as well as I'd hoped.'

'It was a complete disaster.'

'I know. But someone had to say it.'

'You made him feel totally unwelcome.'

'I just wanted to get him home. Talking to his mum, at least. They're missing him so much, Orson. And it's not on, going from house to house. You know that. You agreed.'

'I know. I just wish I'd done it myself.'

Click to see previous comments

OrsonSwell Look, Jake, it's not acceptable to
TOTALLY MAKE UP STUFF that my mum and I
are meant to have said in our kitchen. Our lives are
PRIVATE and you are VIOLATING that, and you can just
SOD OFF. Not everything is about you. I'm sorry you're
homeless and haven't got a career anymore but YOU
ARE NOT A GOOD PERSON JUST BECAUSE YOU
HAVE PROBLEMS.

JakeBenn Orson, could we just talk?

MsKate I'd just like to make it very clear that we had
Jake to stay for nearly a month, and offered him food
and a futon to sleep on (a very comfortable futon, I have
slept on it myself when the twins were sick). We are a
busy family of five, living in a small flat. We value our
privacy. I have not given permission for our lives to be
fictionalised. I would like no further mentions of any of
our household, or I may have to consult a lawyer.

Tammi♥Jake OMG, you'd sue Jake? When
he's had such a hard time? You are a true
witch-beginning-with-B.

MariaBenn Kate, I am so sorry. And so grateful for
the way you looked after Jake. I don't like the way this
series is going, Jake. It's not just your family anymore.
I've tried to complain to the people who run YouTube,
but they say there is nothing they can do. I've got so
many other things on my hands. So sorry. Maria x

JakeBenn Orson, if you'd just reply to my messages? You could appear on the show – have your say?

OrsonSwell JUST LEAVE ME ALONE, YOU ATTENTION-SEEKING FREAK.

Click to load more comments

EPISODE 20

Jake is the only passenger on the top deck of a London bus. It's night. He's been sleeping, but he wakes up with a start.

As the bus drives through north London, a recorded voice calls out the stops.

'Merrivale.'

'I mustn't fall asleep. Mustn't. Someone will see me and they'll take a picture, or they'll steal from me, or I'll end up at the end of the line and then ...'

'This bus terminates at Cockfosters.'

'I don't know anything about Cockfosters. I've never heard of such a stupid name. Orson would think it was hilarious. Orson's not on a night bus at 3 a.m.

'I'm just hoping I can get on another bus and come straight back into town, because it's freezing outside and it's warm on the bus, and I haven't got anywhere to go tonight.'

'Tregenna Close.'

'I just didn't want to ring anyone and have them say no.

'I've got my Oyster card for the bus, I've got my lunch card for school. I've got a cash card for an account which has £200 in it.

'I haven't got any cash though, and I don't want to use that £200 so I need to go to school tomorrow, to eat something and wash and feel like a normal person.

'Huh. What is a normal person anyway?

'I haven't been there all week. I've been off the grid. I didn't want to go to my home, and I didn't want to go to anyone else's.

'And I can't face Mum now that Dylan's got the Prince Jasper job. I haven't heard officially, but I'm sure he has.'

'Oakwood Station.'

'There won't be any trains now. The night bus was full of people when I caught it at Trafalgar Square. They've all got off, one by one. Only a few left now.'

'Peace Close.'

'There goes another one. All these people finding their way through the night to the place where they belong, and I don't feel ... I don't have that.'

'Cockfosters Road.'

'I'm just so tired, but I mustn't go to sleep.'

'Freston Gardens.'

'I can say the whole Prince Jasper speech now. I can remember every word.

'I'd tape it on my phone and send it to the casting director if I had any battery left.

'Maybe I can charge it up tomorrow at school.

'If I go to school.

'But even so, what's the point. Dylan's got the job. Must've got it. I'm sure he's got it.

'I told Orson he had, because he kept on asking and I just thought it'd be easier if I gave up hoping.

'I'm such a failure. I can't even tell the truth anymore.

'I don't want a charged up phone, because then people can ring me. Mum. Zoe. Dad. And I'd have to read their texts and messages. And it'd all be in my head, Dylan getting the part, and no more Riley, and why is there no money anymore, and where am I going to sleep?

'I ought to go home, but home isn't home anymore.

'There's nowhere to go.'

'Cockfosters Station. This bus terminates here. Cockfosters Station.'

Click to see previous comments

ConcernedMum What I don't understand is why your parents didn't just turn up at your school and insist that you came home with them. That's what I'd do.

LizzieK What, kidnap him?

Caring I'd be on the phone to social services if it were one of my kids. Or the police. I'd report them missing.

LizzieK But he wasn't missing, was he? He was going to school.

MariaBenn We thought about it. Believe me, we thought of everything. Neil's stress levels were through the roof. It wasn't a good time.

We talked to the school, and they said that Jake was turning up and doing his work. I phoned round the mothers of his friends – if I knew them – and asked them to encourage him to come home. But we worried about bad publicity. And we didn't want social workers getting involved. And we kept hoping that it was just temporary. We were trying to sell the house. We knew that then we could pay Jake back, and he might come home.

Although there was still the problem of sharing a room. And that flat has never felt like home. Once you've had a nice house, it's hard to accept anything less.

I suppose I'm lucky that Adam doesn't really notice the difference. There are blessings.

Click to load more comments

EPISODE 21

Angela Rose's flat. Jake's asleep on a sofa, covered with a duvet. Angela's making coffee for Logan Winters, who's wearing a towelling gown.

'It breaks my heart, Logan, it really does. My darling Jake, freezing on the street, looking like a homeless person. I couldn't believe it when we came out of that club and saw him huddled on the pavement in Piccadilly Circus. Anything could have happened.'

'Sounds like he's not been home for a while.'

'But why? He's got a lovely mum of his own. Didn't see her much on set, but I think that's because she was working.'

'I fell out with my parents when I was about his age.'

'Did you, darling? What happened?'

'My stepdad was a bastard, that's what happened. So I started staying at friends, and then in a hostel for a bit. And then, well, there are some exploitative people out there, that's all. People who offer you somewhere to stay, but they expect something in return.'

'Oh, Logan, sweetie, I'm so sorry.'

'It's OK. Anyway, somehow I got a place in a hostel. And then I started doing a bit of modelling. Then acting. And then it all took off. I got *Pirates of the South Seas* – and then *Brackenberry Hall*. Now, here I am.'

'With your own flat and a good income and everything's fine now, isn't it, darling? Except one thing.'

'I know. I just don't know how to do it.'

'It's not fair to anyone, Logan.'

'You don't have to tell me that.'

Jake wakes up, blinking in confusion.

'Ange? What? How did I get here?'

'You were wandering around like a lost soul, and Logan and I came out of a club and we kidnapped you. Bundled you into a cab and brought you here. Frozen half to death you were. And now you're going to have a shower, and I'm going to make you a cup of tea and you're going to tell me all about it.'

'I should be at school. And shouldn't you be filming?'

'Saturday, darling. We all get a day off, although I wouldn't put it past that Marcus to call us in at the weekend. Honestly, people think we have an easy life, but it's harder than doing a show every night with two matinees a week. All those pages to learn! I'd like to see Meryl Streep have a go.'

'I don't mind learning pages.'

'I know you don't. You've always been more professional than actors twice your age that I could mention. This one for example.'

Angela nods towards Logan, who is dressed, wearing a hat pulled down to his eye line. He's wearing glasses too. He looks nothing like the man that Whoops! *magazine readers voted Hunk of the Year, three years running.*

'Hey, Jake. Feeling better?'

'I'm OK.'

'Better than me then. There's a steel band playing inside my skull. Remind me never to go out drinking with this woman again. She's pure evil.'

Jake's looking from Angela to Logan.

'So are you two really . . . together? Kirsty always said so, but I never thought it was true.'

Angela and Logan laugh.

'That Kirsty! She's been leading you up the garden path. Logan, I can't believe you haven't told Jake.'

'Look, Ange, a secret is a secret, innit?'

'But Jake's your brother.'

'My *real* brother doesn't even know.'

'Yeah, but that's what's great about being in a soap. You get two families, and they pay you for it. You can tell Jake.'

'Jake, I am not sleeping with Ange, gorgeous though she is. I'm sleeping with Hamza.'

'Hamza?'

'Yes, Hamza. You see the problem? If we come out as a couple, then fans of *Market Square* are going to have a huge shock. And Hamza's family prefer him to keep his private life private. And my family are bigots, who'd hate him for being gay *and* Muslim. And it'd all be played out in the media, and frankly it's easier not to.'

'Yeah, but there's nothing wrong with being gay.'

'You'd be surprised. A lot of bigots out there. A lot of women who'd feel betrayed because they think they're in love with me. And besides, why should we? It's our lives. We're just actors, nothing important.'

'Shush, you.'

'Jake, mate, if you need somewhere to stay, you can always kip on our sofa. I never want to hear that you're out on the street again.'

'Thanks, Logan. It was just an accident. I thought I'd be staying at a friend's.'

'Well, remember. Hamza would say the same. And now I'm going to get the tube over to see him, before he's so pissed off with me that he decides he's not gay anymore.'

'Oh, Logan, he'd never do that. He's devoted to you.'

'I hope you're right, Angie. Bye, Jake. Take care, bruv, OK?'

Left alone, Angela hands Jake a mug of coffee. She waits patiently while he gulps it down.

'Right. Now, in *Market Square* I'm the worst mother on earth, and in real life I've never had kids because heaven help them poor mites, I'd be the world's worst, but I'm going to do my best here. What is going on?'

'I left home. It just got very difficult, and I couldn't take it anymore. I haven't worked out finding a place to live yet.'

'So where are you living in the meantime? Don't tell me you're dossing down on the streets? What about school?'

'No. Mostly I stay at friends'. It's just that they're all a bit fed up now and their parents are asking questions.'

'I bet they are.'

'I don't feel at home anywhere.'

'And what's wrong with going home?'

'My dad's kind of stressed out. And they spent all my money, and they couldn't pay the mortgage, so we had to move into a flat. My brother, he's got health problems.

Autistic spectrum and more. It's kind of driving me mad, sharing a room with him.'

'Oh, honey. That's bad. What about your parents? Why can't they get jobs?'

'Mum has got a job, part time at Tesco. And Dad had a job, but he was so stressed there, and he messed it up. He lost his temper with his boss, and they sacked him. Well, they made him resign. And he didn't get redundancy or a reference or anything. So now he looks after Adam, that's my brother. But Adam's really hard work.'

'Oh, sweetie. This is no good. You need to come back to *Market Square*. Honestly, I could wring Marcus's neck.'

'I think he's going to give the part to someone else.'

'I should call social services. They might find you accommodation.'

'No, Angie, please don't. Mum would be so upset.'

'You need a home. And you can't stay here. It's a one-bedroom flat. There's my cottage in the Cotswolds, but that's no good for you. Tell you what, you help yourself to some food, and I'll do some research. Find out what's on offer. Maybe I can find a friend with a spare room? The problem is though, that I suppose your parents could object. Say you've been kidnapped or some such nonsense.'

'That's crazy!'

'And you'd have to find some rent anyway. You always seem so grown up, we forget you're only ... what, seventeen? Eighteen?'

'Sixteen.'

'Well. Let's find out what the council could do for you. I'll phone their housing department. And then we'll give your mum a ring.'

Click to see previous comments

Housingworker Glad to say that in our area we've seen a real drop in the numbers of younger people asking the council for help with housing. We have a Positive Pathway and are able to help 23% of the young people who approach us. Must be doing something right!

Anna What about the other 77%? What about the ones who never approach you in the first place?

Hilary I was like you, Jake. I couldn't cope living at home anymore. My mum had left and it was just me and my stepfather, and then he moved his girlfriend in, and it wasn't good. I didn't feel safe.

So I went to the council, and eventually they put me in a Bed & Breakfast. Not a nice one, not a holiday place. A tiny little room, with bright orange flowery wallpaper, with big, black blotches of mould. The carpet was full of holes. There were holes burned in the duvet, and the only lighting was a fluorescent strip. The bathroom was down a long, dark corridor, and I was sharing it with ten others. Men and girls. It was rank.

I cried every night I was there. In the end I got onto
a council course, and got a childcare qualification
and a live-in job as an au pair. So, technically I wasn't
homeless anymore. But there's not a day goes past that
I don't think of how it felt, all alone in that place. And
what's more, how easy it'd be to go back there.

Click to load more comments

EPISODE 22

Jake and Maria, sitting on a park bench.

'I know this is difficult, Mum, but hear me out. Things can't go on as they are. I can't rely on mates and I can't come home. It's too difficult, with Adam and Dad. But the council won't help me unless you do this – so I'm asking, please, you just need to write me a letter, saying that you don't want me living with you anymore.'

'Over my dead body! Why would I do such a thing?'

'So that the council will find me somewhere to live. A room or a hostel or something.'

'Why would you want to live in a hostel? You can live with us.'

'Like I said, Mum. It's too difficult. We'd end up hating each other.'

'We love you, Jake, we want you back home.'

'It's just a letter, Mum. It's just words.'

'What if the press got hold of it? Can you imagine the headline? "Is this Britain's Worst Mother?"'

'Mum, people do this all the time. That's how kids get help from the authorities.'

'Well, I'm not doing it. Neither are you. It's a lie. You have got a home.'

'Our relationship has broken down.'

'Our relationship has not broken down. I'm here, aren't I? And if we didn't have our hands full with Adam every damn second of the day, we'd be round your friends' houses, on your case 24/7. What's happened there? I thought you were staying with Orson?'

'I sort of outstayed my welcome. I felt awkward there. I wasn't part of their family.'

'You're part of our family.'

'That flat isn't home.'

'What is home? It's with the people who love you.'

'It's not, though. Nonna loved us, but she didn't live with us. Soon I'll be grown up, working as an actor and travelling around, and you'll be quite happy that I don't live with you. It's normal. People grow up and leave home; they don't live with their parents forever.'

'You're sixteen, Jake. You're not grown up.'

'I feel grown up. I've been around adults forever. I work like an adult, why can't I live like one?'

'Getting housed in a hostel, that's not living like an

adult. That's desperation. Look, I've been thinking, I can share with Adam. Then you and Dad can share, or Dad could sleep on the sofa.'

'Mum, can you imagine Dad's stress levels?'

'I've talked to him about that. Told him he has to get help. He's going to see the doctor. Maybe anti-depressants can help.'

'Why is he like this? He never used to be.'

'I know. He's lost, Jake. He hasn't got a job anymore. He feels like he isn't much of a man anymore. Not a husband or a dad. He needs a job to feel whole again.'

'But it's his fault he hasn't got a job.'

'I know. He shouldn't have lashed out, but his boss was bullying him for months. Piling on the work, picking fault, making your dad feel small, threatening him with redundancy . . . He just couldn't take it anymore.'

'He never really liked his job anyway.'

'You know he wanted to be a musician. He was in a band. He gave it all up when Adam was on the way, so he could be there for me, get a proper job and provide for his family.'

'I know it's hard for him.'

'Imagine, Jake, if that was you. If you had to watch Dylan and Kirsty and all of them climbing the ladder, becoming stars and following their dreams, while you're working in Human Resources.'

'They might not become stars!'

'But your dad's band did. That's difficult for him.

Whenever he switches on the radio and Dog Biscuit are playing, it hits him in the gut. Every time.'

'He ought to get over it.'

'Come home, darling. Please. Dad will work on his moods, I promise.'

'Mum, it's not just his moods. He took everything I'd earned. And he said he didn't want me at home.'

'We had to ... we had to survive, Jake. We were taken by surprise when *Market Square* stopped paying you. We had a huge mortgage, we were so scared of being home-less. Dad didn't mean it. You know he just says things.'

'He did say it though.'

'I know. I'm so sorry, darling.'

'Mum, please just write me this letter.'

'Won't you just try coming home?'

'I can't.'

'Do you know what it feels like to be the mother of someone like Adam? Someone who never speaks? Who turns his head away when you try and communicate with him? I feel rejected, every single day.'

'He can't help it. He's not really rejecting you. And I'm not rejecting you. I just don't want to live in our family anymore. It's not personal.'

'Of course it's personal.'

'It's about me, not you. Can't you see that?'

'Adam changed. That's what makes it so hard. We had a glimmer of what he could be, what he really should be like, and then he disappeared. But he was still there. Like something from a fairy-tale. Someone had put a spell on him, a curse. Taken him away, but left his body for us to care for. And now you've changed too. I thought I could rely on you.'

'I thought I could rely on you!'

'I'm sorry. I'm so sorry. Can't you forgive us? Is it all about money?'

'You know it isn't. It's about me. I need to find out who I am, if I'm not going to be Riley. And I can't do that with Dad bullying me all the time.'

'He doesn't mean to bully you. He's just so tense.'

'He might not mean to, but that's what he does. Please, Mum, just let me go.'

'I'm not writing a letter saying I don't want you at home.'

Jake stands up.

'Fine. I'll just have to cope on my own.'

Click to see previous comments

Anna Nearly half of people living in homelessness accommodation are aged between 16 and 24. That's shocking, isn't it? I think it's not enough to tell your story, Jake. I think you should be giving links to charities that people can send money to (www.centrepointroom.org.

uk, for example) and also providing a helpline number for anyone affected by this. (Shelter's helpline is 0808 800 4444.) Because this is not just a story about some celebrity, or some soap opera. This is real. This is happening to young people every day.

MarketSquareFan We're straying a long way from the original purpose of this series, which was to give something back to the fans of *Market Square*! Our beloved soap has been torn from us. I need to know what was going to happen next. I'm getting desperate here. Please can you give me some answers?!

Click to load more comments

EPISODE 23

Jake is sitting on a park bench in central London. He doesn't see the group of girls approaching him.

'Oh my God! Oh my God! I don't believe it!'
'It's only ... Riley! It's Riley Elliott!'
'I think I'm going to faint!'

Jake looks up.

'It is. It's him!'
'Riley!'
'Jake!'

Jake's appalled, but manages a smile and a wave.

'Ask him for a selfie.'

'You ask.'

'No you . . . you ask.'

'Oh my God! I'm going to wet myself.'

'Tammi!!!!'

Jake gets up to leave.

'Jake, can we have a selfie with you? Please?'

'We're huge fans. We love Riley.'

'Please?!'

'Look, it's just not . . . not the right time, OK?'

Jake starts to walk away. The girls follow him.

'Oh, Riley. Please?'

'Please, Riley?'

'We'll leave you alone . . . just one selfie . . . '

Jake stops.

'OK. Just one selfie.'

'Thank you!'

'Thank you so much.'

'We really appreciate it.'

Jake smiles and poses, but his legs buckle, and he has to grab Tammi's arm to steady himself.

'Oh my God. Are you alright?'
'He's going to faint!'
'Call an ambulance!'

Jake shakes his head.

'No, I'm OK. Not ill. Just a bit dizzy. I'm hungry, but I haven't got any money – my, uh, my wallet was stolen. I don't suppose you've got any gum or anything?'
'Oh, wow! We can do better than that.'
'We're just going to get breakfast. Why don't you come with us?'
'Please let us buy you breakfast? OMG!'
'That'd be great, girls, thank you so much. I wouldn't normally—'
'We'd love to!'
'That's amazing!'
'Let's go!'

The scene changes to a cheap hotel room in central London. Tammi is asleep on a bed. Jake is sitting beside her. He speaks to camera.

'Look, it's not what you think.
'They were really nice, and they bought me breakfast and then they said I could use their room – this room – for a shower and a sleep, a chance to charge my phone. I said I'd had a rough night. I didn't go into details.

'They weren't here. They were going to Madame Tussauds, to see the waxworks. Look, here's a flyer they brought back. A two-hundred-year-old attraction. It moved to Baker Street in 1835. Says here: "Visitors paid sixpence to meet the biggest names of the day."

'Except they weren't meeting them, were they? They were meeting big lumps of wax.

'It's kind of weird, isn't it, that people still go to Madame Tussauds. I mean, back in 1835, fair enough, there weren't any films or TV, or photos. If you wanted to see a celebrity you had to get up close, or see a portrait or something.

'Now they visit so they can take selfies, and pretend they've met Barack Obama or Prince Harry or whoever. But then what?

'Maybe they wanted to feel that celebrities were human. Maybe they wanted to touch them. It's a kind of ownership, isn't it? I see this person, and I touch something that looks like them, and they belong to me.

'Even though you're just touching, seeing, photographing the equivalent of a fancy candle. Even though if you burned the lot of them you'd just have a pool of melted wax.

'I think it's creepy.

'I went to Madame Tussauds a few years ago. *Market Square* was the top soap then – awards, viewing stats, everything. It was amazing. They made a big display, and the Elliott family were part of it, we were the centre of it.

'And I remember looking at the model of Riley and

thinking how weird it was that I'd grow and change and he wouldn't. That people who'd never meet me would visit him. That Riley was something separate from me, a character that other people owned. The viewers, the writer, Marcus.

'I mean, it's sort of obvious now, but I was only thirteen.

'And I have no idea if the waxwork Riley is still there or if they've melted him down to make some boy band's body parts.

'Or maybe he's in some storeroom somewhere, dusty and dirty and covered in cobwebs.

'Anyway, I was asleep and Tammi must've come in while I was sleeping. Nothing happened. I'm sure I would have remembered.

'I'd better just check her phone.'

Jake reaches across Tammi for her phone. Just as he's stretching across her to pick it up, his phone rings, waking up Tammi and startling Jake so he falls on top of her. Tammi shrieks. Jake tries to roll off her, and she grabs him.

'Oh, Riley. This is my dream!'
'I'm not Riley. He doesn't even exist.'
'He so does. We visited him at Madame Tussauds.'

Tammi grabs her phone.

'Look. So cute.'
'Ugh. So young.'

Jake quickly flicks through the rest of Tammi's photos.

'Oh no, don't delete them. I want to show everyone.'
'You don't need all of them. Look, I'd better be going. Thanks, um, I can't remember your name ...'
'Tammi! It's Tammi. Don't go. I ... we ... well, we tossed a coin for you, and I won. But if you prefer one of the others ...'
'No, no, really it's OK.'

Jake retrieves his phone.

'Look, my agent just called. Could be important. I've got to go.'

Tammi's eyes fill with tears.

'Oh God, don't cry.'
'I'm sorry, it's just when I saw that coin come down tails, I thought, I hoped ... but never mind.'

Jake hesitates. He checks that Tammi's phone is back on the side table. Then he leans forward and kisses her on the lips.

'Tammi, it was special. I'll never forget it. But I've got to go. I've got school.'

Exit Jake.

Click to see previous comments

Tammi♥Jake OMG. OMG. You had her play me? Really? First, it was much more romantic than that. I swear. That kiss went on, like, forever.
Second, she's a fat cow. Must be size 16 at least. Get in shape, girl, you're disgusting and going to die way too soon. I could see that Jake hated kissing you.

DestinyRock Shut up with your insults. I am just playing a part. Jake wrote the script. You have no right to body-shame me. I'm proud of who I am and what I look like. For your information I am extremely fit. I do Thai kick-boxing. You'd better not get in my way.
Also, I have no interest in kissing Jake Benn, other than for dramatic purposes.

Click to load more comments

EPISODE 24

Jake's at school, in a drama studio with Destiny, Orson, Tom, Manon, Freya and Fabienne.

'So basically, you've done nothing? No ideas at all.'

'Aw, leave it out, Destiny. Stop with the nagging. It's only drama.'

'Orson, if you don't think drama's interesting, why are you even doing it?'

'I dunno. Thought it might be less rubbish than textiles.'

'Yeah, right. You just wanted to do it because of Jake.'

'You what?'

'Because without your celebrity mate, you're nothing but a pathetic show off.'

'And you're so popular, aren't you? I wonder why.'

'I don't care about popularity! I care about the performance we're going to give.'

'I tell you what we could do. We lie around on stage and you tell us off.'

Orson imitates Destiny.

'You're all so lazy and useless! Why don't you work hard like me? I'm just so superior to all of you.'

'Shut up, Orson.'

'Jake?'

'She's not wrong.'

'I can't believe you're standing up for her. She's just a self-satisfied swot.'

'Destiny, tell us what we were meant to do.'

'Research. Gathering material. I went to an old people's home at the weekend.'

Orson yawns.

'Bet that was thrilling.'

'It was, actually. They were very interesting. One lady told me about the war . . . about working on a farm . . .'

'So exciting.'

'Shut up, Orson.'

Orson shuts up. But he's glaring at Jake and Destiny.

'So that's what we've got to do? Talk to old people?'

'Well, if you'd been at the briefing meeting we had three weeks ago, Jake, you'd know that we decided to do two groups. Old people and the homeless. Obviously it's more difficult to get hold of homeless people to interview, but I've thought of a way ...'

Destiny's voice fades out. Jake's looking away.

'You taking the piss, Destiny?'

'Shut up, Orson.'

'No, I mean it. Pretty insensitive, eh?'

'What do you mean?'

'Well, you know ...'

'No idea. Explain yourself.'

'Well, it's just—'

Jake stands up.

'Shut up, Orson. Just shut your big mouth. No one's interested, OK?'

'Mate. Calm down.'

'I am calm!'

'No you are not. You're frothing at the mouth.'

'Just shut up, OK. Shut up with your banter. Shut up with your jokes. Shut up with your stupid comments every two minutes.'

'Talk about ungrateful.'

'What the hell?'

'You basically invaded my house, and now you're telling me to shut up? When I was trying to speak up for you?'

'I haven't invaded anything. I don't need you to do me any favours.'

'Yeah, right. We've been feeding you, washing your clothes, putting up with the way you smell—'

Jake launches himself at Orson. They wrestle, bumping into a studio light and bringing it crashing to the ground.

'Stop! Tom, Freya, help me make them stop.'

'Leave them to it.'

'Yeah, Destiny, none of our business. Let's go.'

'But I can't just . . .'

Exit Tom and Freya, Manon and Fabienne.

'Stop! Orson! Jake!'

Jake shoves Orson away from him, with more violence than before. Orson staggers into a corner, and slides to the ground. No one's laughing.

'You know what, Jake? You thought you were some big shot because you were an actor, but now you're just like the rest of us.'

'What?'

'You're nothing special. You've got to start giving as well as taking.'

'Take that back.'

'It's true, you know.'

'Shut up!'

Orson stands up.

'I'm going. And forget staying at mine tonight. Or ever. I'll bring your books in tomorrow.'

Exit Orson. Jake turns away, so no one can see his face. Destiny hesitates by the door.

'Jake, I . . . I'm sorry. I didn't realise.'

No answer.

'I'll just go. I'm sorry. Bye.'

Click to see previous comments

OrsonSwell Totally out of order.
I don't care that it was six months ago. You have no right.
You just twist everything. I was standing up for you! I was telling her that she was insensitive!

But no, now she's your best friend, and I'm the enemy.

Piss off, loser.

Click to load more comments

EPISODE 25

A café in central London. Jake's sitting at a table, eyeing the menu. Enter Zoe, his agent.

'Jake! How are you, darling? I've been worrying about you.'
'I'm fine. Absolutely fine. Never been finer.'

A waiter arrives.

'Espresso. Thank you. Jake?'
'Oh, I'll have ... eggs. And toast. And crushed avocado, and artisan sausages and organic mushrooms. Also orange juice. And a croissant.'

The waiter leaves. Zoe's looking at Jake.

'Truly? Never been finer?'

'Yup.'

'Well, your parents are not fine. They've called me almost every day since the audition. Have I heard from you? Have I heard about the part? Can you re-do the audition? Do I know where you are?'

'Oh. Sorry.'

'Do I know where you are? Why are your parents asking me that?'

'I've been staying with friends.'

'And the casting director's assistant called too. Are you OK? Are you under too much pressure?'

'Dad's not good with stress, and sometimes it all gets a bit much for him.'

The food and Zoe's coffee arrive.

'I know your dad takes your career very seriously. I know he can be very intense. But it's no more than that, is it? He's not . . . you always seemed such a happy kid. I know you enjoy what you do.'

'I do enjoy it.'

'I remember you at the British Soap Awards, getting Best Newcomer – you were sparkling that night. Your mum and dad were so proud. So was I.'

'I know. I mean, thanks.'

'It's been hard losing your gran, hasn't it? She was a wonderful support to you, as chaperone, and going to all the auditions.'

Jake stops eating. He's blinking back unwelcome tears.

'I do miss her. It's just lots of things, really. My dad lost his job. And my brother, he's quite hard work. It all got on top of Dad, worrying about money and everything. It's not his fault. I just need to get a job, as soon as possible . . . just to have some money.'

'Jake, do I need to call social services?'

'No, don't do that. Please don't.'

'I don't want you in any danger.'

'No, I'm not.'

'I don't want any pictures of you looking like a down-and-out.'

'There won't be.'

'And obviously I care very much about your welfare.'

'Yeah, obviously.'

'Jake, they haven't decided 100 per cent about that part. Prince Jasper. They'll see you again, if you're up for it. Dylan hasn't signed a contract; apparently his parents are causing trouble, seeing if they can fit filming around his exams. I could have a word.'

'I don't know.'

'I'll get someone from the agency to take you if they want to see you again. Or you could go by yourself if you prefer. You're sixteen now, you don't need a chaperone.'

'I don't?'

'No.'

'Can I take charge of my own career? Like, you pay me any money I earn direct?'

'I'm not sure. You'll need to talk to a lawyer.'

'Oh. OK.'

'Is that what you want? Independence from your parents?'

'Yes. No. I don't know.'

'Jake, this sounds serious.'

'It is serious. I am serious. I want to be in charge of my own life. I'm sixteen, and I've been working for ten years. Surely I've earned the right to make my own decisions?'

'I'll look into it, but I don't hold out much hope. We had another client … they didn't get very far. This isn't America; you can't divorce your parents.'

'Really?'

'Really. I think being more independent would involve you being taken into care. The courts would have to agree … there would be a lot of publicity.'

'And even then I'd just be swapping my parents for some other adults?'

'I think so. I can try and find out more.'

'Don't bother, it's not worth it. Thanks for breakfast, Zoe. Let me know if there's any news. I've got to go to school.'

'Thing is, Jake, I have got some news.'

'What news?'

'You've got to see it as good news, darling. Doors opening not closing. New opportunities.'

'You mean – Riley?'

'So many child actors get typecast.'

'They don't want me anymore?'

'You have *huge* potential.'

'Zoe! What happened?'

'They're doing a live show, sweetie. I got the details from Marcus yesterday.'

'A live show?'

'I know. Exciting, eh? But I'm afraid it's bad news.'

'Riley?'

'They've given the part of Riley to Bobby.'

'Bobby?'

'Bobby Broadbent. He's reinventing himself as an actor.'

'He's not ... he doesn't even look like me.'

'They'll dye his hair, do their best with make-up ... '

'I can't believe it!'

'I'm so sorry.'

Click to see previous comments

BobbyBroadbent Just want to make it clear – again! – that I didn't steal Jake's role. The producers of *Market Square* came to me.

I did it partly to work with Kirsty. I love that girl. I don't care who knows it. I still don't understand why you chucked me, Kirsty. Please give me another chance.

So anyway, what I wanted to say was, sorry, Jake. I never meant to nick your job. I took it as a career opportunity. And because I wanted to be near Kirsty.

Sorry, Kirsty. I love you, darling. I love your crazy laugh and the way you twirl spaghetti round a spoon.

I love the way you sing songs from musicals when you're in the bath. You've got a great voice.

I love your jokes, even though I never get them.

Won't you take me back?

KirstyConnor No. Please stop harassing me in public. If it happens again I am going to the police. I would ask Destiny to remove your comment, but I want it to stay as evidence. Inappropriate behaviour. Go away!

Click to load more comments

EPISODE 26

St Peter's Church food distribution for the homeless.

Some people have asked to remain anonymous, so we have pixelated their faces.

Thank you for helping us with the making of this series.

Please watch out for the information at the end which tells you how to donate to this cause.

A small crowd of people surround the volunteers handing out food. Denise and Ian are distributing soup and sandwiches.

'Here you are . . . one for you . . . tuna alright, Ian? How are you, my love?'

The homeless people take their food.

'Here you go, darling. How are you, Kayleigh?'
'I'm OK.'
'Any luck with a hostel place?'
'Nah. I hate it there. Don't feel safe, you know?'
'It's all wrong, a young girl like you out on the street. That's not safe, Kayleigh.'
'I can look after myself better on the street than in a hostel, Denise. Can I have some more soup?'

Denise ladles another cup of soup. She spots Jake.

'How about you? Haven't seen you before, have I?'
'No.'
'New on the streets? Have you talked to anyone? Your local housing department?'
'He won't get any joy from them, Denise. You're living in a fool's paradise if you think they'll house him.'
'He's very young, Ian. Are you eighteen? If not, they have to find you something.'
'I'm fine. I'm OK.'
'You're not OK if you're here. I'm Kayleigh. I can help you.'
'I'm OK, thanks. Just a bit hungry.'

'Denise means well, but she don't know what it's like. They put you in some shitty hostel or a B&B, and if you don't like it, if you can't take it, then they don't do no more.'

'Why not?'

'Voluntary homeless, they call it. Voluntary bullshit.'

'Mostly I'm staying with friends. But sometimes it's hard to find someone.'

'What about your parents? Can't you go back home?'

'No. Maybe one day. But not now.'

'You don't look like you belong here, mate. You look like you should be home with Mummy and Daddy.'

'Yeah, well, I . . . '

Denise is staring at Jake.

'Don't I know you, sweetheart? I'm sure I've seen you before.'

'Denise, none of us have never seen him here.'

'But I know that face!'

'No, I don't think so.'

'No, he's never been here before. I know everyone. I know everything too. You just left home? Stick with me, I'll see you right.'

'Kayleigh, he ought to see the council. Get himself a place in a hostel, or one of those charities.'

'You know what happened last time I tried a hostel, Denise? It was bitter cold, last winter, and I turned up late, and they said, nah, full up, can't help you. Here's an Oyster card, they said. It's all paid up for a few days. Go and find yourself a night bus. That'll keep you warm.'

'That's shocking.'

'That's true. Come with me. I'll show you where we sleep. It's not pretty, but it's safe.'

'I'm OK.'

'Are you? Because you don't look it. And you don't want to get help from just anyone. We've all got to look out for ourselves.'

'I . . . OK.'

'You come with me.'

Click to see previous comments

LizzieK I'm sorry, but just wondering, what about Dylan? Why didn't you go and stay with him?

JakeBenn I should've done, I know. His family have a big house and everything. But he's in north London and that's miles away from my school or home. And somehow . . . I didn't want to call that group of friends. The acting ones. They know me at my best, and this was my worst, and I felt too embarrassed to admit I needed help. I've changed a lot since then.

LizzieK And didn't your school notice what was going on? Didn't your schoolwork suffer?

JakeBenn Yeah, they were on at me a lot. Meetings

and detentions and interventions and all that. I didn't put it in the show because, you know. It's boring. We all know what schools are like. This is a dramatisation, not a documentary.

LizzieK So, Kayleigh, is she real? Or made up?

JakeBenn She's a sort of mix up of several people I met around that time. People with awful stories. Brave, broken people. And I wanted to let people know about them, but I didn't want to take their privacy away from them. So, newspapers, if you want to run stories saying 'Jake's story doesn't stand up' and call this series a 'carefully concocted tissue of lies', go ahead. I know it's true.

Click to load more comments

EPISODE 27

*Jake's in a makeshift camp under a bridge by a canal.
All around him people are sleeping. Kayleigh's nearby
in a sleeping bag.*

Jake, to camera.

'It's raining. If it wasn't, I'd just leave. I'd rather walk
and walk than sleep here.

'It stinks. The worst smell you can imagine.

'You can hear traffic noise all the time, and something's dripping – can you hear it? It's enough to drive
you mad.

'These people live here. Dave, there, he's slept under
this bridge for six months. Chris, he's been here a year.
How is that even possible?

'I couldn't do it. I can't do it. I'd just chuck myself into the water. Even though it's full.

'I'm thinking, why don't I just go home? Sharing a room with Adam – it's nothing, compared to this. Nothing.

'There would be food, and it would be warm, and, you know, they really care about me. Even Dad. Especially Dad, in some ways.

'But I feel like I don't deserve it. This is what I deserve.

'I've let them down. I'm not good enough.

'I've got nothing to contribute anymore. No money. No work. Nothing to make anyone proud of me.

'Nothing to feel proud of myself for.

'I'm not Riley anymore.

'I'm not going to be Prince Jasper.

'If I can't act, what am I? Who am I?

'I am nothing.

'Nothing.

'No one.

'Nothing.'

PART 4

This above all: to thine own self be true.

Hamlet, Act I, Scene 3.

EPISODE 28

Thank you for your kind donations. You can also
help the homeless by donating to Shelter and
St Mungos.

---

*Back at the church. Denise is handing out sandwiches
again. Jake is at the back of the crowd, hat pulled
down, looking as unlike Riley as possible.*

'Here you are, darling. How are you?'
'I'm alright. Thanks.'
'What about me, Denise? Don't give them all away.'
'Don't worry, Kayleigh. Plenty for you tonight.'

*Kayleigh grabs her sandwich, starts eating. She's
looking at Jake.*

159

'You're back? What happened to you? You found some-where to sleep? You didn't like it under the bridge?'

'No . . . yes . . . not really . . .'

Kayleigh laughs.

'You scared of me?'

'No.'

'I know it's a shithole, that place we stay. But it's our shithole, OK?'

'Yeah, sure.'

'I don't need you putting it down.'

'No. I know. Look—'

'Jesus, who's that girl?'

Destiny has approached Denise, and is waiting to talk to her.

'She doesn't look like your normal . . . What's the matter? Seen a ghost?'

'No, I . . . I need to get out of here.'

'What's the hurry? You were going to tell me where you're staying.'

'No, I . . .'

Destiny spots Jake.

'Jake?'

'Oh hell, no.'

'Jake?'

'She knows you?'

'Shhhh ...'

'Jake? Jake? Oh my God!'

'It's not ... I'm not ...'

'What are you doing here?'

'I'm – I'm not ...'

Denise stares at Jake.

'Riley Elliott, that's who you are!'

'Who?'

'Little Riley. Off *Market Square.*'

'No ... I mean, I'm not—'

'You are! I love that show. Kayleigh, did you ever watch *Market Square*? Isn't he Riley?'

'I hate that show. Load of toss. My foster mum, one of them, she loved it. I can't remember Riley. Was he the whingy one? The one that was dealing drugs and training to be a ballet dancer?'

'No, that was Jamie Arbuthnot. His family moved to Scotland ... OK, I used to be Riley.'

'What are you doing here, then? A bit of research?'

'No, I ...'

'You're rich, you're famous. You can buy your own food!'

'I'm not ... I'm sorry Kayleigh ...'

'You should pay for that sandwich. Pay me, not Denise! I'll give you all the research you want. Want to know what it's like to sleep on the street? Or to stay in some-one's house because you're desperate, but they want stuff from you . . . all sorts of things. And you do it because you can't stand the thought of another night in the cold and the rain, until they go so far that you think you'd prefer to be outside all night every night?'

'I, I'm sorry—'

'Want to know how it feels to have no family? No one who cares about you? No one who'd notice if you were alive or dead, except a few guys here on the street, and Denise here, who likes to be a do-gooder because she hasn't got any kids, and she's in a shitty job and giving us food makes her feel like her life's worth living.'

'Kayleigh!'

'Jake, I don't understand. Are you here to do research?'

'Shut up, Destiny. Leave me alone!'

'You think you can come here, maybe spend a night sleeping out, and it's some big adventure, an experience, and it's all fake emotion for your fake life.'

Jake's had enough.

'You don't know anything about me, Kayleigh. You don't know why I'm here.'

'You're angry with me? Now I've heard everything.'

'I'm not doing research. I'm here for my own reasons.'

'Yeah? Well you are one sick individual. Because if I'd earned loads of money on some television show, I wouldn't be taking food from the homeless. For any reason. I'd stay at home and eat my supper and use my iPhone and watch films on my tablet, and lie down in my nice, soft, warm bed and sleep. I'd sleep for hours. And I'd invite a few people to stay in my house who didn't have homes of their own as well.'

'OK, I get the message. I'm going.'

'No you're not.'

'Kayleigh, let go of him!'

'You're going to pay for the food you took.'

'I can't!'

'You can.'

'Let me go!'

'Find the money.'

Kayleigh lets go of Jake's arm. Jake pulls a two-pound coin out of his pocket.

'Here, have this. Leave me alone.'

Kayleigh takes the coin. Pockets it.

'Nice one, mate. Thanks a lot.'

Jake walks off. Destiny follows him.

'Jake, I'm so sorry. I was doing research for our GCSE. I'm so sorry.'

'Just leave me alone, OK? I'm not doing the GCSE. I'm not coming back to school. I'm all on my own, and that's how it's going to stay.'

'Jake, you should come back to school. Please, Jake, come back?'

'No. It's a waste of time. Leave it, Destiny, OK? Just leave it.'

Jake walks off. Destiny follows him.

'You can sleep on our sofa tonight, if you want? Come on, Jake.'

'No. Thanks, but no.'

'OK, meet you here tomorrow at four? After school? I'll bring food. Jake?'

Jake doesn't reply. Destiny's left on her own.

Click to see previous comments

CaringMum I don't blame that girl Kayleigh for being upset. You should have gone home to your mother.

Tammi♥Jake Or come to Leicester to stay with ME! Any time, Jake.

JakeBenn I was thinking about trying again at home. I'd arranged to go round to Arthur's that night. But he was out 'til late and I had no money, and I was starving. It was only a sandwich. Not exactly filling.

DenisePJones Speaking as the volunteer who gave you that sandwich, I can confirm that we don't ask for referrals when we hand out food at night. We take the view that if you're asking, you're probably in need. I'm sorry if I embarrassed you. I don't judge anyone who comes to us. There but for the grace of God, that's what I say.

And I hope you don't mind me saying something a bit political, but the people we serve are getting a whole lot younger.

Click to load more comments

EPISODE 29

Destiny is waiting for Jake on a bench opposite the church. She's got a large bag of food with her, a sleeping bag and a flask of coffee.

She's looking at her phone, about to give up. Then, just as she's getting up to go, Jake arrives.

'Jake! I didn't think you were coming. It's really late, and you weren't at school.'

Awkward silence.

'I brought you some coffee. Here, it should still be warm ... And food. Look, doughnuts!'

Jake grabs the doughnuts and coffee.

'Careful ... I mean, you don't want to choke. I just think you need somewhere to stay. You need to get help. Why can't you go home?'

Jake shrugs. He's searching around in the bag for more food.

'I asked my mum, but we just don't have any space. It's me and Mum and my little sister, all in a two-bedroom flat, and the second bedroom is really small, and it's got my mum in it. There's the sofa, but it's not a long-term solution.'

'It's OK. We're not even friends.'

'I know that. It's just ... I mean, no one should be living like this.'

'I cracked last night. Rang my friend Dylan. You don't know him, he's an actor like me.'

'Dylan Johnson? I've seen him on the TV.'

'Yeah. So I rang him. He's busy with this and that, out with friends and talking about auditions and work and ... all things that should be my life, you know? All things that are mine, or were, or ... I just don't know where I am anymore.'

'So did he say you could stay with him?'

'I couldn't even ask. I know he's got a spare room but his mum would ring my mum, and that'd be difficult.

Then everyone would know. Everyone in my world. I can't let that happen. I don't know what to do.'

'Why can't you go home?'

'Lots of reasons. Mostly my dad.'

'What's happening with your dad?'

'He's ... he's stressed. Angry. He's sort of scary when he's like that, and he doesn't realise it.'

'I had a dad a bit like that. My mum left him. We never see him anymore. She changed our names as well as our address. My name was something different then.'

'I didn't know ... didn't realise ...'

'So do you think your mum might leave your dad?'

'No. She loves him, and he's not that bad. They have to look after my brother. They're stuck together, whatever happens.'

'No one's stuck together forever.'

'Feels that way. We're a unit, a family, a group. It's just that I can't take it anymore. I don't want to be at home.'

'Home should be a launching pad, not a prison.'

'That's very profound.'

'One of the old ladies said it to me when I was doing that research.'

'I should've come with you.'

'Well. You've had other things on your mind, I can see that. I'm sorry it caused a fight with Orson.'

'It's been waiting to happen. It's not his fault. I've been taking our friendship too much for granted.'

'I'm sure he didn't mean it.'

'I don't blame him. I've been sleeping at his house on and off for weeks now.'

'Jake, I've got an idea about where you could stay. It's a bit risky, but it might work. My mum's a cleaner, and she goes once a week to this woman's house. She's a really old woman – she's got Alzheimer's or dementia, or something. She's gone a bit cuckoo, Mum says. Anyway, she lives all on her own with just some carers visiting. No family or friends, just a lawyer.'

'How could I stay there?'

'The house is huge. I could bring you food, and sort out stuff like clothes. Maybe get one of your entourage to help – Arthur, maybe? He seems quite intelligent. Get yourself sorted and you can start coming back to school, and working towards the exams, and things will get better.'

'But what . . . I can't just walk in there . . .'

'Honestly, you can. I've got Mum's key. And the lady's asleep most of the time.'

'It's a mad idea. What if she sees me? What if she calls the police?'

'She won't. She's in her own world. Jake? Are you up for it?'

Jake doesn't say anything. But slowly he nods his head.

We would like to stress that Destiny's mum knew
nothing about this idea at all.

Comments have been disabled on this episode.

EPISODE 30

Jake and Destiny are out on the street, watching as an old woman in a wheelchair is wheeled out of a large red-brick house. As soon as she and her carer disappear around the corner they run for the front door, let themselves in and go up the stairs.

Destiny opens a door to a darkened room, full of mahogany furniture.

'This is amazing, Destiny.'

'You'll need to keep the curtains closed. It's a bit dark and dusty.'

'I don't know how I'm going to get away with it though. Isn't it against the law?'

'It's not really strictly legal, but you're not hurting

anyone. You'll just have to be careful going up and down the stairs, and in and out. Mum doesn't do these rooms often. No one uses them, you see.'

'But what about when she does? What if she finds my stuff here? Or me?'

'I thought of that. There's a cupboard there, with a key.'

Destiny shows him an ornate wardrobe in the corner.

'Put everything in there and lock the door. If you sleep in a sleeping bag and make the bed in the morning, she won't notice. She comes here in the middle of the day on Fridays. You'll be at school, won't you?'

'Yeah.'

'Promise?'

'OK, I'll come.'

'And we can use some of your experiences for GCSE drama? I have to get something together soon, no one else is going to.'

'Oh. Alright then. Nothing too personal though.'

'OK, deal.'

'I might not even do my GCSEs. They want to see me again, for a film. I screwed up, first time round, but there's still a chance.'

'I could help you prepare for it, if you want. Did I tell you I want to be a director one day? Film or theatre, I don't care.'

'I never knew that.'

'I know it's going to be difficult. Mum thinks I should stick to nursing or something like that. Be a midwife, or a computer programmer.'

'Why?'

'Because working in the arts is so insecure.'

'Nothing's exactly secure. My dad was working for an insurance company and he had to make loads of people redundant. And then he lost his job as well.'

'That's what I said to my mum. You've got to make your own luck. So anyway, as far as I can work out the carers come three times a day, four days a week. Morning, lunchtime, evening. Keep out of the way then.'

'But what about the old lady?'

'As long as you don't wander around, you'll be OK. And I was thinking, you can do your washing in the launderette, and have a shower at school, in the changing rooms.'

'I can't do that. The PE staff will think I'm really strange.'

'We'll have to ask Arthur then. Maybe you can use his house.'

'What am I going to eat? And how?'

'You can have breakfast and lunch at school. Evenings, you can get something at Arthur's, or at mine. Or buy a Subway or something.'

'But I haven't got any money. Not for the launderette or Subway or school lunch or anything. That's why I went to the church to get food.'

'You're going to have to get a job.'

'A job? But I've been trying to get a job. I can't. There aren't many auditions for people my age, and the film is a really long shot and anyway the money would go to my parents.'

'Jake, I mean a real job.'

'A real job?'

'Maybe in a shop, or babysitting. Or walking dogs. In a café. Cleaning. You know, the sort of things that normal people do.'

'Oh. Oh, I see what you mean.'

'I can ask around if you want.'

'OK. Right. OK.'

'Maybe there are people you know that you could ask? Maybe television people need cat-sitting or dog-walking or something.'

'Do you think I could teach?'

'Teach?'

'Well, I used to go to a performing arts class when I was a kid. That's how I got into it in the first place. Maybe I could go there, offer to help out. I'd like that.'

'You could try. Did you really think that acting was going to keep you in full employment for the rest of your life?'

'No ... well, not full employment. Enough to live on.'

'Yeah, well, I don't think it works like that. In the meantime, I can lend you a fiver.'

'Thanks, Destiny. Really appreciate this.'

'Just don't get caught. It'll be fine.'

Click to see previous comments

CaringMum It really is disgraceful that squatters are now treated as criminals in our society. What are homeless people meant to do? Houses lie empty and people sleep in the streets, and no one cares. Well done to Jake for highlighting this problem!

Londonlandlord It's clear you have no idea at all of the hazards of owning buy-to-let property. The law has to protect the rights of the owner, or we have chaos! I own several buy-to-let flats, one was taken over by a group of squatters who lived in filthy conditions and caused massive damage. You can't just live wherever you want to! It cost thousands in legal fees to have them ejected.

Bystander Jake isn't exactly a squatter. He's moved into a house where the owner is still living, without asking for permission. I'd call that breaking and entering.

DestinyRock We didn't break anything! We used a key.

Bystander A stolen key.

DestinyRock We weren't doing any harm. And if the owner had known, I think she would have said yes.

Click to load more comments

EPISODE 31

Jake is in a large sitting room, filled with bookcases, a bed at one end of the room and a winged armchair at the other. He's looking at a large portrait of a woman.

'This is a strange way to live.

'A sort of half-life.

'I can sleep here, but I wake up a lot, lying there, worried that someone's going to find me.

'I'm scared that the old lady will stumble across me. She'll be so shocked that she'll have a heart attack and die.

'They'd lock me up.

'So today I didn't even try and go to school. I waited until they took her out, and then I came downstairs to have a look at where she lives.

'I was just going crazy in that room. I was too scared to leave it, but every time I needed the loo, I had to. Just across the corridor . . . and then flushing it made a noise. A huge noise. I was sure someone would hear.

'Maybe she did hear. Maybe she thinks I'm a ghost.

'A fat ghost who's eating too many Subways and too many flapjacks.

'I've been watching my weight for ever, feels like. You get very aware of your body when you're going to auditions; people are looking at you, judging you on how you look. A lot of the time that's what it comes down to – what you look like. People say girls are the ones obsessed with their looks, but it can happen to anyone. My face, my body . . . if I get fat, it limits me. Maybe it means I'd get other parts but, you know, who wants to be Augustus Gloop? Or Dudley Dursley?

'Actually, right now I'd happily bulk up for either of those parts. I'd do anything to be working. I don't feel right without a part to prepare for. All those years being Riley, weekly scripts, working so hard. There's a huge gap.

'I don't think they really want to see me again for Prince Jasper. Dylan's got that part. They're just sorting out the details. They're being nice because of my dad. And I couldn't nick it from Dylan anyway.

'I suppose I got complacent. All those actors I met who told me about being out of work, I just never thought it would happen to me. Some of them do tutoring or dog-walking, or house-sitting. They work in cafés and pubs and shops. I used to hear about it and think, oh well, that won't be me. I'll always have work. I'm so far ahead of the competition. I've got savings. I'm famous already and I'm only a kid.

'I was an idiot.

'Anyway, I'm acting a part here and now. The invisible man. No one can see me; I've worked out when the carers come and go, more or less. I spent a whole day just lying here, listening to the door opening and closing, to people talking in the hallway, trying to work out what they do when they're here.

'They cook a bit in the downstairs kitchen. They talk to the old lady, all bright and loud and false. They must help her get clean and dressed, I suppose. I don't know what she can do, how much she can look after herself.

'I watched out of the window for a whole day, working out when the carers came and left, and if anyone stayed overnight, which they don't. But one comes very late and one turns up early in the morning, which means that going to school is much more difficult than it should be. I have to wait until they go into her room and then do a stealth dash to the door. I've got good at opening and shutting it in complete silence.

'I'm sure this will come in useful for a part one day. Something that's about hiding and staying still and quiet. A war film maybe, or spies. I wish this was a film. I wish someone would shout "Cut" and I'd be finished for the day.

'This house is full of stuff. Pictures and books and clothes and rugs. Old-fashioned toys, a rocking horse, a piano. It's like being on a film set just waiting for the actors to arrive. It's beyond sad. But it also makes me angry, to see all this unused space when people are living on the street.

'I think she was an actress, the lady in this room. There are theatre posters in frames. She's got shelves full of plays – Shakespeare and Marlow, Brecht and Shaw. I wonder if she'd mind if I borrowed some to read? I could put them back later. I don't think she'd notice, would she? It's not stealing if I don't take them out of the house.

'It's a bit like living with Adam again, except there's no *Thomas the Tank Engine*, and with Adam I could see him, talk to him, watch his responses, try and work out what was going on in his head.

'I miss Adam. I miss his noises. I miss his silence

'I even miss *Thomas*.'

EPISODE 32

Destiny, Arthur and Jake, in school uniform, outside their school.

'It's not that I'm not grateful – I am, you guys are brilliant. It's just more difficult than we thought, that's all.'

'Yeah, but it's better than the street though.'

'Yeah, obviously. Anything's better than the street. But I'm not getting great quality sleep.'

'But that bed looked so comfortable.'

'I'm not sleeping in the bed. I feel a bit exposed. Like, what if someone came in the room when I was asleep? I'm sleeping on the floor behind the bed. So no one can see me.'

'Who's going to see you? The old lady probably can't even come upstairs. She's always in a wheelchair.'

'She's in a wheelchair to go outside. She wanders around downstairs. I've seen her. And she might have a carer staying overnight, or someone from her family. Or anyone, really. I mean, if I'm there, someone else could be.'

'You're mad.'

'Sorry, but I'd rather get some sleep on the floor than no sleep in a bed.'

'OK, but everything else is working, isn't it? You've worked out when you can go downstairs? You're getting enough food.'

'Yeah, but some things are difficult. Like, for example ... well ...'

'What?'

'Well, using the loo. Don't laugh. It's awkward.'

'There's one right across from your room, I showed you!'

'Yes, but it's really noisy! It's so old fashioned – you pull the chain, and it's like bang, crash, creak, creak ... I can't do it.'

'What do you mean, you can't do it?'

'I just can't. Someone will hear.'

'Yes but just wait until the carers aren't there.'

'And what about her? The old lady? She'll tell them there's someone in the house.'

'She won't be able to check.'

'Arthur, she'll know. Ghosts don't poo.'

'Jake!'

'It's true! Fictional characters don't either. In three years on *Market Square* there was never one character who went to the loo. Ever.'

'Yes, well understandably so. I can't even believe we're talking about this!'

'No, it's important.'

They haven't noticed Neil approaching them.

'Jake.'

'Dad!'

'I need to talk to you, Jake. It's been weeks now. It's tearing us apart.'

'Jake, we can wait for you.'

'It's alright, guys. I'll ... I'll just see you tomorrow. Don't worry.'

Destiny and Arthur leave. Neil sits down next to Jake.

'I suppose I should thank you for talking to me.'

'No, Dad, it's OK, you don't have to—'

'I don't know what I have to do. How can I make things alright, son?'

'I don't know.'

'How can we get you to come back? I accept I've messed up. I accept I've pushed you away.'

'You didn't, it was me as much as anything. I just couldn't take it, living in the flat, sharing with Adam.'

'You think we should send him away? To some institution?'

'No, I'm not saying that.'

'Maybe it will come to that.'

'But Mum, she'd never forgive herself.'

'She could work longer hours. I could do something – drive a cab maybe – and earn money. We'd be able to pay you back. You could come home.'

'It shouldn't be a choice. You shouldn't have to give up Adam for me.'

'Isn't that what you want us to do?'

'No way. Adam wouldn't be happy if he was just sent away from all of us.'

'He's not happy now. He misses you.'

'I miss him. I miss everyone. I miss working as well. And I'm never going to work again if I have to live in that flat.'

'It won't be forever.'

'Why not? What's going to change?'

'The house is on the market. When we sell it we'll be able to pay you back.'

'But you've got a huge mortgage! That's crazy, Dad, you won't have anything left.'

'Do you think I don't know that?'

'You'll be living in that flat forever.'

'This isn't helping, Jake.'

'I'm trying to get more work. I'm so sorry about *Market Square*. I know we relied on what I was earning.'

'You shouldn't have to worry about this, son. You're the kid and I'm the adult. I ought to be the one earning the money. If I hadn't lost my job ...'

'You couldn't help it.'

'They were making me redundant anyway. I even messed that up. We would have had a lump sum at least.'

'Dad ... it's OK. I'm OK. And I will be able to help again one day. Just let me get my exams out of the way.'

'You're having to grow up too fast. I'm so sorry.'

'Dad, I've felt like an adult ever since I started working. It's a relief to get there at last.'

'I'm so angry about *Market Square*. So angry with that Marcus, playing god with our lives. For no reason. You were doing a good job. You were popular. You deserved to be paid more, not suspended.'

'It's OK, Dad, don't worry about it.'

'I'd like to ... never mind. Let's leave it. So, where are you living?'

'I can't tell you.'

'I'm your father!'

'You've got enough to worry about. I'm OK, I've got somewhere to stay.'

'And you're in touch with Zoe? And she might have auditions for you?'

'Yeah, maybe. She might. Don't worry. Everything's going to be OK.'

Click to see previous comments

JaneThompson I hope you don't think I'm intruding,
but I do think your parents seem very isolated with
Adam. Have they had him assessed recently? Have they
looked at the services available? Things have moved on
since he was little, and they might be surprised at what
he could achieve, particularly having moved to a new
borough – the support might be different.

BenTaylor I've got an idea about your problem going
to the loo. Why don't you get those plastic bags my mum
uses for the dog?

Click to load more comments

EPISODE 33

Jake in the bedroom of the house where he's staying, later the same day.

'My timing's all wrong, and I haven't eaten anything. Dad was trying to get me to go back home, but all my stuff was here in the cupboard, and I sort of wanted to go, but also I didn't. I couldn't. I knew if I saw them, saw Mum, I'd feel even lonelier when I got back here.

'This is so awkward.

'I'm starving.

'I've had three biscuits in the last seven hours. I know I need to lose a bit of weight, but this is ridiculous.

'The last carer has gone. No one else comes until 7 a.m., according to the rota Destiny got from her mum.'

Destiny's mum knew nothing about this.

'I could go downstairs. There must be some food in the kitchen. But what if she's there? What if she sees me?'

There's a sound, a faint voice. Someone crying.

'Oh, God, what's that?
'It must be her. Is she hurt?'

Jake picks up his torch, creeps down the stairs. The crying is getting louder, and he can make out some words.

'Oh, my lovely girls, my babies. Where are you? Where has he taken you?'

Jake freezes, in the hallway. Then he pushes the door open, switches on the light.

'I'm sorry. Don't be scared – I heard you, and I thought . . . I thought . . . '

The crying stops. The old lady sits upright in bed, staring at Jake.

'What time do you call this? You're late!'

Jake is completely shocked; the torch falls out of his hand. He slowly inches into the room.

'I ... I'm sorry ...'
'Most unprofessional! I expect precise time-keeping for an audition.'
'An audition?'
'Well that's why you're here, I presume?'
'I ... I suppose so ... I thought you were crying ...'
'Crying? Nonsense! Go on then, let's hear you.'

Jake swallows.

'Could I have a drink of water? My mouth is a bit dry.'

Marguerite gestures towards a side table with a jug and glass.

'Help yourself.'

Jake takes a drink.

'Is there anything you would like me to read?'
'Whatever you have prepared.'
'Oh. OK.'

188

Pause, while Jake thinks his way into the Prince Jasper speech.

'I have trained as a swordsman with the finest blades in my father's kingdom. I have jousted and wrestled and lifted weights. I might look young, but I am strong and healthy. But this – I have never been treated like this. A prince of the Dark Isle, set to shovelling latrines.

'If he were not your father then I would order him executed, strung up by his neck like a puppet on a string. But I cannot. Because that would hurt you, and your sweetness is worth so much more than his harshness. Can't you see that? Can't you see that your much beloved father is evil? His evil will be pardoned. I promise you that when I am released, I shall be merciful.'

It is the best performance of the role that he has given. Jake's elated.

Marguerite shakes her head.

'I don't know this text. I like the way you read, though. I'll give you another chance.'

She points a bony finger towards the bookcase.

'*Hamlet*. Third shelf from the top. Find it.'

Jake picks up his torch and manages to locate the copy of Hamlet.

'Any page will do. I want to hear you speak some Shakespeare.'

Jake starts reading, stumbling over the words.

'O that this too too solid flesh would melt,
Thaw, and resolve itself into a dew!
Or that the Everlasting had not fix'd
His canon 'gainst self-slaughter! Oh God! God!
How weary, stale, flat and unprofitable
Seems to me all the uses of the world.'

Marguerite leans forward.

'That was awful. Terrible. Weary, stale and flat, indeed.'

Jake's slightly annoyed.

'I was just reading it through. I don't actually know the play at all.'

'Well, get to know it. And that speech in particular. It'll do as an audition piece. Come back in ... hmm ... two days. Fully prepared.'

'I will. Two days. That's Saturday.'

'Two o'clock. And this time I expect you to be punctual.'

'But you'll have someone here with you then. A carer.'

'An assistant, possibly. That shouldn't stop you.'

'I . . . is it OK? I've been sleeping upstairs.'

'Well, that's more usual than sleeping downstairs, or outside. What is your point?'

'It's just, it's your house . . . '

'You need proper theatrical digs. Plenty of land-ladies out there. But until we have cast you, you had better stay where you are. As long as you do not bother anyone.'

'No, I won't, I promise. It's just . . . I am quite hungry . . . '

'Help yourself, my boy. Plum pudding and leftover turkey in the pantry, I think you'll find.'

'But it's not Christmas.'

Marguerite laughs.

'Well, of course it's not Christmas now. Now it's New Year. And lucky for you, because we always have a houseful at Christmas. Now, leave me alone. I have to sleep.'

'I . . . of course. Thank you.'

'Saturday at two. Don't forget.'

'I won't. Thank you. Thank you so much.'

Click to see previous comments

JakeBenn I just want to thank Edie Lombard for agreeing to play Marguerite. I asked her because we were in that film together – *Picking Daisies*. I was her grandson. She's always been an inspiration for me. I never thought she'd agree to be in a web series, but she did. I'm so grateful.

DestinyRock I'm more than grateful, I'm still in shock! I, Destiny Rock, have directed Dame Edie Lombard. Edie Lombard! Not that she needed any directing, but she was so gracious, so wonderful. And so exactly like Marguerite!

MarketSquareFan I'm sorry, but are we ever going to hear about the storylines just left dangling? It's preying on my nerves ... I can't sleep at night. Just some closure, that's all I need. Someone must be able to help me, surely?

Click to load more comments

EPISODE 34

*Two o'clock in the afternoon. Saturday. Jake comes
downstairs. He looks nervous. He knocks on
Marguerite's door. Karoline, the carer, answers.*

'Who are you? How did you get into this house?'
'I'm here for my audition.'
'Audition? Like on *X Factor*?'
'Sort of.'
'Who are you? How did you get in? The house is meant
to be empty!'
'I'm ... I'm staying here. I have permission. And she
asked me to come here at 2 p.m. to have an audition.'
'Permission? From who can you have permission? She
asked you? I don't think so.'

Karoline steps aside, so Jake can see Marguerite.
She's sitting in her armchair, staring into space. She's
completely still, not listening to their conversation,
disconnected from the world around her.

'She did, honestly. She's not always like this.'

'She is always like this. I come here four days a week.
I talk to her, wash her, feed her. She never says one word
to me. She never asks me for an audition.'

'I can't explain it.'

'How did she ask you in the first place? And how long
are you living here?'

'Just for a few weeks ... I'm not sure ... Look, I'm not
meant to be living here. I haven't got official permission.
But she did ask me for an audition, and I sort of think,
even if you throw me out, it feels important to do that for
her. For me as well.'

'I'm going to call the police!'

'Look – did you ever watch *Market Square*?'

'*Market Square*? Yes ... we even had that in Poland.'

'Well, don't you recognise me?'

'You?'

'I'm Riley. Riley Elliott.'

'Riley! Sweet little Riley!'

'I'm not so little anymore.'

'So, what are you doing here? Are you family to
Marguerite?'

'No, not really ... '

194

'Well, having you here is good news for us carers. You can keep an eye on her when we are not here.'

'I'm happy to do that.'

'She shouldn't be left on her own so much.'

'I know. That's why I want to read to her. She's expecting me, I'm sure of it.'

'How can she be expecting anyone? She doesn't know what's going on.'

'Just let me ... please?'

'Well, alright then. Riley. I can't believe it!'

Jake walks into the room, and stands awkwardly in front of Marguerite. She doesn't seem to notice him.

'So, I'm back. Saturday at two, like you said. For my audition. I've been learning the speech from *Hamlet*. The notes in the book, they were very helpful.'

No response from Marguerite.

'OK, well, I'll just start then.

'O that this too too solid flesh would melt,
Thaw, and resolve itself into a dew!
Or that the Everlasting had not fix'd
His canon 'gainst self-slaughter! Oh God! God!
How weary, stale, flat and unprofitable
Seems to me all the uses of the world.'

Marguerite stirs in her chair.

'Fie on't! ah fie! 'tis an unweeded garden,
That grows to seed; things rank and gross in nature,
Possess it merely. That it should come to this!
But two months dead: nay, not so much, not two:
So excellent a king; that was, to this,
Hyperion to a satyr; so loving to my mother
That he might not beteem the winds of heaven
Visit her face too roughly. Heaven and earth!
Must I remember? why, she would hang on him,
As if increase of appetite had grown.'

Jake stops. He waits. Karoline takes out her phone.

'I really should phone the agency.'
'Wait, please . . . '

*Slowly, Marguerite's face starts to move. Her mouth
opens and closes. Her hands lift from her lap and
reach out to Jake. He hesitates, then takes one hand.*

Karoline can't believe what she's seeing.

'She's trying to speak. What's she saying?'

Marguerite's voice is little more than a whisper.

"Tis an unweeded garden,
That grows to seed; things rank and gross in nature,
Possess it merely.'

Click to see previous comments

   LizzieK I had no idea you could act like that.
Extraordinary.
   CaringMum And Dame Edie too! This should be on
TV!
   Tammi♥Jake I'm in pieces!
   ZoeM I'm very proud to be Jake's agent, and I'm sure
you'll agree that this series is showing a whole new side
to his talents. Please don't hesitate to contact me if you
would like to speak further about future productions.

Click to load more comments

EPISODE 35

Edie Lombard, speaking to camera.

'I knew her, you see.

'Oh, not very well. She must be fifteen years older than me at least.

'But Marguerite Morgan! To be so utterly forgotten – it's unthinkable.

'So many people my age lose themselves. They start struggling with words, and then they drift further and further from us. Poor Marguerite. Lost in a world of ghosts and shadows.

'People have found it strange that I would involve myself with a web series.

'Lucky me, I have been very successful, and I am not

starving like so many in my profession. And I applaud the boy, Jake, for making art out of misfortune.

'And you know, he's really a very talented young actor. I have suggested that he should try and go to drama school. I know that some of the younger actors think they can learn on the job but I think a proper training is necessary. If only for the contacts.

'I understand that young Destiny, who is here to film today, is also keen to have a career in film or theatre, as a director. You should follow your dreams, my dear.

'I followed my dreams, from the backstreets of Whitechapel to the West End stage.

'And Marguerite followed hers, from a farm in Ireland.

'She was born Maggie O'Halloran, and her father wouldn't hear of her going on the stage. He thought it was a shameful thing for a young girl to hanker after. But she ran away, and she went to London and she made it happen.

'It wasn't easy then and it isn't easy now.

'But a dream is a dream, and life is all too short.'

EPISODE 36

Marguerite's house. Destiny's in the hall with
Karoline. She's clearly nervous.

'I'm Destiny. Jake said it would be alright . . . I brought
him some food.'

'Hi Destiny, I'm Karoline. Jake is in with the old lady.
I don't like to disturb.'

'So, let me get this straight . . . you're OK with Jake
being here?'

'Jake being here is a good thing. Miss Marguerite was
so lonely before. And now she has someone to work
with.'

'To work with?'

'It is a miracle.'

'A miracle?'

'Come and see.'

They go into the room where Jake is sitting with
Marguerite. Jake leaps up when he sees Destiny.

'Destiny! You won't believe this. She can talk – she's fine.'
'Well, Jake, not really fine—'
'Don't listen to Karoline. Come and listen to us.'
'What's going on?'
'We are in rehearsal, Jake! Where have you gone?'
'I'm sorry, Marguerite, I'm coming. Destiny, just listen.
It's amazing.'

Jake re-joins Marguerite. He's learned his lines now.

'And therefore as a stranger give it welcome.
There are more things in heaven and earth, Horatio,
Than are dreamt of in your philosophy. But come;
Here, as before, never, so help you mercy,
How strange or odd soe'er I bear myself,
As I perchance hereafter shall think meet
To put an antic disposition on—'

Marguerite interrupts.

'What do you think antic means?'
'Old – you know, like antique—'
'Wrong. Antic means mad. Hamlet's going to pretend

to have a mental breakdown. He's feigning madness – for what purpose?'

'To take revenge?'

'Indeed. But what do we know about Hamlet?'

'He's already a bit mad. Sad. Depressed.'

'Correct. But antic is a different sort of madness. It's the happy mask, not the sad one. He's putting on a show of craziness – clowning around. In Shakespeare's time people would be familiar with the idea of a mask in theatre, actors putting on clownface, shall we say? So there's also a joke here at the expense of actors. Hamlet is pretending to be something he's not – but it's also something that he might be. So, how are you going to say that line?'

Jake considers.

'More like this . . .

'As I perchance hereafter shall think meet
To put an antic disposition on,
That you, at such times seeing me, never shall,
With arms encumber'd thus, or this headshake,
Or by pronouncing of some doubtful phrase,
As "Well, well, we know," or "We could, an if we would,"
Or "If we list to speak," or "There be, an if they might,"
Or such ambiguous giving out, to note
That you know aught of me: this not to do,
So grace and mercy at your most need help you,
    Swear.'

'Much better. You're getting the idea. Let's think about how your arms are encumbered.'

'Jake?'

'Who have we here? Our Ophelia?'

'Yes! That's a brilliant idea. Destiny, you'll read Ophelia, won't you?'

'Jake, what is going on?'

'She's ... she's directing me. In *Hamlet*. I don't really know ...'

'But she's meant to be really old ... my mum said she's got dementia.'

'She's not ... it's fine.'

'Young lady! Are you going to read Ophelia or not? Please do not chatter. We have a lot to get through if there is going to be a performance next week.'

'Next week?'

'I don't know ... she comes out with stuff.'

'Jake ... do you think it's alright? Should we be doing this?'

'It's fine! It's good! It's like ... like the best thing I've ever done.'

'Karoline?'

'Ophelia?'

'I'm coming. Just preparing ...'

'I work sometimes with other old people. They were happier in the old days than now. They get confused ... can't keep up ... and then something reminds them of the past, music maybe or a person, and they are happy again.'

'Maybe she was a director? Or an actress?'

'I think there are many books of plays on her shelves.'

'I want to know!'

'Ophelia?'

'Jake, I can't be Ophelia. Ophelia doesn't look like me. She's meant to be all delicate and droopy, not ... well ... not like me. Not black. Not big-boned. Not taller than Hamlet.'

'Come on, Destiny, you're the one who's going to be a director. Who says Ophelia has to be anything? She's what you and Marguerite make her.'

'You won't laugh?'

'I never would.'

'Alright. Where's the book?'

'Here—'

'O, my lord, my lord, I have been so affrighted!'

Click to see previous comments

MarketSquareFan My mother, before she passed, she couldn't recognise us. She didn't know my name anymore. She didn't know her own grandchildren. She couldn't remember words for things. Ordinary everyday things. Eggs. Keys. Beans.

She was weak as a kitten. She couldn't cut up her own food. She couldn't wash herself or dress herself. She'd been an active, working woman all her life – a dinner lady, a cook – and by the end she was an empty shell. A ghost of herself.

But she could tell you the name of every single character on *Market Square*. And talk about them as though they were neighbours. For half an hour, three times a week, she was normal again. She was laughing, she was talking, we had something to chat about. Something to keep a sense of her alive.

Then she died. And *Market Square* was a way of remembering her. But then *Market Square* was pulled. And now there doesn't seem much point to life at all.

CaringMum Are you alright, love? I'm a bit worried about you.

Click to load more comments

EPISODE 37

Marguerite is on her own, still in her chair.

'Well, this is a strange play.

'People come in and out and they don't say much and I can't make out all their words.

'Muttering. Mumbling. It's the modern way and I don't like it.

'Sometimes I think I recognise people, but mostly not. Bad acting. Unconvincing.

'And tedious. Nothing to take my interest.

'I pity the audience.

'Maybe I am the audience?

'I don't know if I'm on stage or in the audience or back-stage, or where I'm meant to be.

'It's like a dream. But it's not a dream. I'm awake.

'I used to know where I was, and how to move, and what my cue was. What's my cue?

'What am I waiting for?

'And I used to be the one who made all the decisions, who held all the threads in my head. Not much room for that now. It's all stuffed up with rags and bones and bits and pieces and snippets of words and faces.

'Snippets. Is that even a word? Snippets. Snip. Ets.

'I'm not sure. I'm not myself anymore.

'Is that what we're waiting for? For me to decide who is who and what is what?

'I remember all sorts now. Life on the farm, with the chores to do, always so bored and my back aching and no fun in our lives, church on Sunday and bread and gravy if we were lucky.

'Mummy telling me to take my chances. My sister Bridie giving me her savings. Bridie had a job, cleaning for the priest. She said I needed the money more than she did. It was Mummy and Bridie who got me away from that farm, got me to England.

'I couldn't fail after that.

'This grand house, it used to be full of people. The parties we had.

'And my children. Where are my children? My beautiful girls.

'What happened to them?

'Who took them away?'

EPISODE 38

Jake's bedroom at Marguerite's house.

'It's not just the acting. That's what I was trying to get Destiny to understand. It's not just that I feel like I've gone up so many levels all at once.

'The words ... and the feeling ... and how she explains it ... and what she expects of me ...

'It's just so exciting! I feel so alive, somehow, like this is what I've been waiting for all of my life. To try something like this.

'I even filmed myself today, just one or two speeches, on my phone. I sent them to Zoe, so she can see what I can do. So much more than just being Riley.

'So much more.

'But it's not just that. I was trying to tell Destiny – and

she got it, she really did, and she was great at being Ophelia, and I'm thinking we could bring more people in, actors, and people from school, and we could do the whole thing. All the parts. The whole play.

'I mean, if just hearing someone read could do this to Marguerite, could bring her back to life, then what about a whole play? With a stage? And an audience?

'She was a director once. Karoline and I ... we went looking. We shouldn't have, but there's a big desk in another room, the front room, the one no one goes in, and we looked in it, and there are letters and things. All sorts. About touring in Britain in the 1950s, and experimental theatre in the 1960s and stuff from the 70s and 80s ... She's nearly 100 years old. No wonder she couldn't remember a lot.

'But she's still in there. She is! All the words, all the thoughts, the ideas, the plays were in her head.

'When she's had enough, she just says "That's it! Rehearsal over for today! We meet again tomorrow." And she goes off to sleep. And that's it. The next day she's back to being silent and old and vacant again.

'But then I pick up the book and read to her, and she's back. She's there!

'And all I want to do is read more.

'But what I want to know is, does this work for everyone? Everyone silent, I mean. Everyone lost. Do you just need to find their thing and try it? Because ... because ...

'Maybe I need to go home.'

EPISODE 39

The Benn family's flat. Maria is in the kitchen. Adam is watching television.

Jake lets himself in quietly, and whispers to Adam.

'Hey, Adam!'

Adam turns and sees Jake. He turns away, buries his face in a cushion.

'Hey, it's OK.'

Adam starts making a moaning noise.

'Shush ... Adam, it's OK. It's me. It's Jake. You remember

me, don't you? You must – it's me, your brother. Look, I want you to come with me. Will you? Will you come with me?'

Jake and Adam stare at each other. Slowly, Jake puts his hand out. Slowly, Adam looks at his hand.

'Come on ... I'll leave a note for Mum. It's OK.'

Adam stands up. He reaches out to Jake. For a moment they stand there, nearly touching. Nearly looking at each other. Then Maria comes into the room.

'Jake! Darling!'

Adam retreats, back to the television.

'Hey, Mum.'
'You're back. Jake. You're back.'
'I'm just visiting.'
'You're just visiting. And are you going to tell us where you've been living?'
'No. I'm fine. Don't hassle me.'
'Don't hassle you? Do you have any idea what we've been through in the last few weeks?'
'I'm OK! Actually, I'm great. I'm happy. I'm over it.'
'You're over what?'
'Everything. Riley. The film part. The money. It's all OK.'

'You're over it?'

'I was really low. I thought I was going mad. But now ... everything's changed. It's OK now.'

'What on earth, Jake? Are you on drugs?'

'No, nothing like that. Really. It's just, I've met someone, and the most amazing thing—'

'Who is she? Is it that Kirsty?'

'No, Mum, nothing like that.'

'Are you living with someone? A girlfriend?'

'No, no, really, Mum. I'm fine. Don't worry.'

'Well, tell me, then. What's so wonderful? Where are you living? Are you ever coming back?'

'I'll tell you soon. We're going to have ... well, sort of a party. Invitation only. I'd like you to come.'

'A party?'

'Sort of. A performance. A play. You'll see.'

'Jake, don't do this to me. You have to come home. We'll sort things out.'

'I'm OK! I just want to borrow Adam ... take him out somewhere.'

'What do you mean, borrow him?'

'Just take him for a walk.'

'Jake, that's not a good idea. You know how difficult it is. He might throw a tantrum, or run away ... it's not good for him, darling.'

'Mum, when did Adam last leave this flat?'

'Well ... I don't know ... it's so difficult now. We had to sell the car ... we haven't got a garden ...'

'You can't keep him prisoner.'

'We're just trying to look after him!'

'Mum, no wonder Dad is stressed. This is no good for anyone. Not for Adam, and not for you.'

'What gives you the right to tell us how to live our lives?'

'I think this might help.'

'You're not taking him anywhere. Not today. He's tired and he's due for his tea. You know how he is about routine.'

'Tomorrow then. Tomorrow afternoon. Please, Mum?'

'Jake, I can't ... Will you stay here tonight? If I let you take Adam out tomorrow?'

'I can't, I've got to get back. I'll come back tomorrow.'

'I know how difficult today is for you, darling. I understand.'

'You what?'

'*Market Square*. Today's the day the new Riley takes over. The live show.'

Click to see previous comments

DestinyRock Just a heads up for the next episode. So far, obviously, we've had Angie Rose play herself, and also Jake's mum, Maria. But in the next episode we're using That Episode of *Market Square*, where Angie's playing Patsy Elliott, but also being herself as well, and it's just too complicated if she's also playing

Maria. And Kirsty Connor couldn't stand in, because she's Poppy Elliott, obviously. So we were left with difficult casting decisions.

We asked Jake's mum if she'd consider being herself, in one scene. And she said she'd give it a go. So a huge thank you to Maria Benn, for supporting our project!

Click to load more comments

EPISODE 40

We start with the actual episode of Market Square. *The BBC has never made it available for viewing, but there are many versions circulating on the Internet.*

Angie is at her market stall, selling a bag of apples and talking to Kirsty.

'I'm worried about Riley, darling. He's been so moody lately. Do you think he's in trouble? Teenagers, nowa-days ... could it be drugs?'

'Well, Mum, actually ... I didn't know how to tell you ...'

There's a noise off screen. Someone is shouting. Angie adlibs.

'Oi! Keep the noise down! Some of us are trying to work.'

A man crashes into shot, falling into Angie's fruit stall and sending everything flying. A security guard follows.

Angie and Kirsty on set, and Maria and Jake watching at home all exclaim together:

'Oh my God!'

Maria clutches Jake's arm.

'Wasn't that . . . ?'
'Dad! It was Dad! I'm sure it was.'
'They cut away so quickly. Straight into another scene.'
'Play it back.'

Maria rewinds. We see the scene one more time.

'It was him. Look – his black jacket! And he was shout-ing something about Riley.'
'Oh, Jake. What has he done?'
'I don't know. Where is he?'

'He could be anywhere. Oh God, they're back again.'

*On the screen we're back in the market with Angie and
Kirsty. The stall lies in ruins around them.*

'Well! Some people. This square ain't what it used to be.'
'No ...'
'So, anyway, darling. What were you going to tell me?'
'Sorry, what?'
'About Riley, sweetheart. About how he's not his old
self.'

*Kirsty starts to laugh. She's horrified. She tries to
speak, but her voice is a tortured squeak.*

'He's certainly not that, Mum. Sorry. Sorry.'

Angie is the ultimate professional.

'Do you think he's on drugs?'

Kirsty pretends she's crying.

'Mum ... Mum ...'

*There's a quick changeover to a different scene. The
actors look startled. Maria and Jake look at each other,
horrified.*

217

'This is terrible.'
'Mum, this is a disaster. And it's all Dad's fault!'

The landline rings.

'Don't answer it, Jake!'
'But it might be Dad.'
'It's not your dad, I can see him. He's under two security guards!'

The phone won't stop until Maria pulls it out of the wall. Jake's phone is also ringing. He switches it off.

On the screen, Logan and Bobby – the new Riley – approach Angie and Kirsty.

'Riley? Darling? You're not looking well, sweetie. Not yourself.'

Muffled shouting in the background. You can just about make out the words 'Not Riley'. Kirsty loses it altogether.

'That's not Riley, Mum, don't you know your own son? That's Bobby. He's not worthy of our family name.'
'Oh! Well! Have you been drinking? Or am I getting confused?'

Logan steps in.

'Don't worry. I can explain everything.'

Everyone – on screen and off – is amazed.

'Well, go on then.'

Logan grabs Bobby's arm.

'I said I was bringing Riley here today, but I didn't. Mum, sis, I can't live a lie anymore. This is my boyfriend; he's called . . . he's called Bobby. And we're very much in love, whether you accept it or not.'
    'Oh, darling! At last. I'm so happy.'
    'Eh?'

Bobby's puzzled face is the last anyone sees, as the Market Square credits roll a full two minutes before its official running time is over.

'He's not Riley. You're still Riley. Oh, Jake!'
    'Mum, you're joking. The entire Elliott family is going to disappear after this!'
    'What do you mean?'
    'They went off script, they just made it up. You're not allowed to do that – it's completely unprofessional.'
    'They did it for you, Jake. Solidarity.'

'They're all going to get sacked, and it was completely Dad's fault.'

'Your dad didn't make them forget their lines.'

'He invaded the set!'

Jake looks at his phone.

'Zoe's already called me three times. I think my career is over.'

'Oh, Jake. Oh, sweetie.'

'I can't believe he did that. Why would he do that, Mum? He's ruined everything. I'll probably never work again.'

'Don't cry, darling. Don't cry. You'll upset Adam. Come here, have a hug.'

'I'm not crying.'

'It's alright. It's alright, Jake. Your dad's not well. I think he needs help. He won't listen to me, but maybe now he will see the damage he's done. I'll tell him. We can't go on like this.'

'Mum, I'm sorry I walked out on you. Do you understand?'

'I do, my love. I do understand. Believe me, I've felt like walking out myself. Neil's turned into someone different. He's not the man I married. I've been so weak, hoping everything would work out. Well it won't, I see that now. Trust me, I'm going to make sure he gets the help he needs.'

'It's OK, Mum, it's not your fault.'

'I miss your Nonna so much.'

'So do I.'

'We've got to think about what she would have done. And she wouldn't just let things get worse and worse.'

Adam takes one of his trains and waves it in Jake's direction. Jake takes it from him.

'Is it for me? Thank you. Wow ... Edward. You don't often give anyone Edward.'

'He hasn't done that for ages. It's because you're back.'

'I'm not staying. I'm not back for good.'

'I know. Maybe one night though? Just one?'

'Oh ... OK then. Just to see what happens with Dad.'

'I'll try and ring him now.'

'I have to go and get some stuff. But I will be back.'

Jake starts playing trains with Adam. Maria goes into the kitchen.

'We'll go another day, to see some trains. I think that trains are to you, what Shakespeare is to Marguerite. And I want you to talk like she did. Because that would just be the best.'

EPISODE 41

Kirsty Connor, in her flat.

'Why did I do it? Why did I commit professional suicide on live TV?

'I couldn't stop myself.

'I panicked.

'They'd cast my ex-boyfriend as my brother. Bobby's not even an actor. It was cynical and stupid and wrong.

'It wasn't fair to any of us, but especially Jake. He'd never put a foot wrong. Marcus was playing god, and someone had to stand up to him.

'I felt like a pawn in a giant game of chess. A piece of Lego. A doll. I was a shadow, playing at being a puppet. Poppy Elliott was sucking out my soul.

'I'd heard about advance storylines – Logan and me,

we got one of the writers drunk one night – and I knew what was going to happen to Poppy. Pregnant with twins. Padded up like a beach ball.

'And then death in childbirth.

'A Christmas special.

'I'll never be trusted again. My agent's sacked me.

'I don't care.

'I do care, but it's too late.

'I'm thinking of teaching drama.

'I'm going to write my own material.

'And I'm definitely going to have a go at stand-up.'

Click to see previous comments

MarketSquareFan This scriptwriter – she didn't let anything else drop, did she? I'm desperate here!

LizzieK Have you thought of trying another soap? I could talk you through *Emmerdale*.

Click to load more comments

EPISODE 42

Jake and Marguerite in Marguerite's sitting room.
They've been rehearsing.

'Much improved. Much improved. I do think you are finally beginning to understand what you are doing.'

'I do think so as well. Marguerite?'

'Yes?'

'Can I ask you – what happens to you ... in your head ... when we're not rehearsing. Do you know?'

'I beg your pardon?'

'I mean ... do you remember? Like, for example, what happened earlier today?'

'Earlier today? Have you gone mad? We were rehearsing. All day!'

'Yes, but ... well ... not really all day. Karoline was here.'

'Who?'

'She comes nearly every day to look after you.'

'To look after me? Do you mean the maid?'

'No, yes ... sort of ... '

'She's here to look after the house, not me. And the children when they come home from school.'

'The children?'

'My children. You must have seen them. Rosalind is the older one and Sophia the younger. No discernible talent at the moment, but it is early days.'

'But they must be grown up now. More than grown up. There aren't any children living here.'

'They are my children, whatever anyone says. They live here with me.'

'What do you mean, Marguerite? Don't get upset.'

Marguerite is trembling. Jake puts an arm around her, tries to calm her.

'He says I can't look after them. That I should not be working. But how can I choose between my children and my work? Why should I? My work is my life.'

'No, no, don't worry, Marguerite. Don't worry. It'll all be alright. I'm sure of it.'

'No one asks a man to choose between his work and his children. No one counts the hours he spends with them, and judges his worth as a father.'

'I know ... it's alright ... '

'No one spies on him, and accuses him of taking lovers.'

'It's OK, Marguerite . . . it's OK . . .'

'Are they still here? Has he taken them?'

'I'm sure they are, they must be.'

Marguerite stands up, frail and wobbly on her spindly legs. She sways a little.

'I must go and see. They should be upstairs in bed.'

'No, Marguerite, you can't go upstairs. You're not strong enough. You'll fall.'

'You don't understand. He's trying to take them away.'

'They're not here! You're old. They must be old too. They're not children anymore.'

Marguerite stands, staring at Jake in silence. She reaches a hand to her head.

'What are you saying?'

'It's just . . . I don't know when you think it is, but you can't possibly have small children. You're quite old now. Your memory isn't working properly. And your children must have grown up a long time ago.'

Marguerite sinks back into her chair.

'You're wrong. Quite wrong.'

'No ... I'm really not.'

'If they are grown up, then why do they never visit me? Where has he taken them? Where are my children?'

'I don't know, but I'll help you find out.'

Jake helps Marguerite back into her chair.

'I can't stay tonight. I promised Mum I'd go back. They've arrested Dad. I don't know if he'll even be home. He's having psychiatric assessments; I think he might have gone a bit mad.'

'But where are they? My girls? Where are they?'

'I don't know. I'll help find them, I promise you.'

Click to see previous comments

LillyM Edie Lombard is such a marvellous actress.

LizzieK I was crying there.

CaringMum I thought Jake's dad was heading for a nervous breakdown. All the signs were there. Terrible for the family. That poor woman, she won't know which way to turn.

JakeBenn In the next episode I'm playing Adam. I'm sorry if it's confusing. I could have let Dylan go on, but I wanted to try and get an idea of Adam's inner life ... his voice. If he had a voice.

I've spent my whole life trying to work out what he

is thinking. So I didn't want the next bit of my story to be just me talking about Adam, or even my writing something for Dylan to act. I wanted to give Adam the voice I think he has.

Click to load more comments

EPISODE 43

Adam to camera.

'I understand.
'More than they think.
'Just because I don't do that thing that they do.
'Noising.
'And eye-wetting.
'And all of it.
'Just because I am.
'Adam.
'Is who I am. And it would hurt too much to take part in their games, and their touching, and their tears and smiles and all of that busyness.
'All of that hurting and noise.
'So much noise.

'And him and her and them.

'Shouting.

'When I have things to watch and do that are calm and quiet and easy and contained. Trains on tracks and into tunnels. Thomas and Edward and James.

'Always the same.

'Easier.

'But.

'He was here and then not here and then here again.

'Brother.

'Jake.

'And he said he would take me outside.

'To trains. Like Thomas.

'And he went away. And he is lost. I hear them saying. Lost, lost, lost.

'All gone lost.

'Like Stepney the engine. Lost in the fog. Went to the scrapyard. The two bad diesels took him to the smelting shed. It was red and hot and a huge grabber came from the ceiling.

'But then the Fat Controller finds him and Stepney says there's no place like home.

'So now I have to find him.

'Outside.

'Jake.

'No place.

'Like home.'

EPISODE 44

Jake and his parents are at their flat, waiting for news of Adam. Neil's head is bandaged, his face bruised.

'It's my fault. If I'd been here, he wouldn't have been left alone. I've ruined everything. I've destroyed our family, I've destroyed Jake's career, I've ruined *Market Square* ... and now Adam ... we might never see him again.'

'It's alright, Dad, it wasn't your fault, it really wasn't ... it was my fault. I talked to Adam about going outside. I thought it might help him. It's my fault.'

'Shush, both of you. I was here with him. I should have seen him go. I took my eye off him, didn't lock the door ...'

'Mum, don't cry ...'

'I've been talking to social workers. Trying to find somewhere for Adam to go. Just a day centre, or a training scheme or something. So he has a life of his own. But maybe he heard me, maybe he thought I was trying to get rid of him?'

'No, Mum, I'm sure he wouldn't.'

'I've turned into a monster. I don't know what possessed me. I'm going to get help, I promise.'

'You're ill, darling. It's all been too much for you. The BBC aren't going to press charges, they're going to help you get better.'

'They are? But how?'

'They said ... maybe a stay at a place for people with problems. They're used to it, I think. Burn out. Breakdowns. I talked to a lovely woman from HR, she was so kind ... '

'I can't go away, I have to stay here for you, Maria. And Adam. We have to find Adam.'

Jake stands up.

'Jake—'

'I'm going out to look for him.'

'But the police said to stay here.'

'You two stay. I can look. I'll find him, I promise.'

Jake leaves.

232

'Jake?'
'Jake?'

The scene changes to Marguerite's house. Karoline lets herself into the house. She finds Marguerite lying in a heap on the floor.

'Marguerite! Oh my God!'

Karoline fumbles for her phone.

'Ambulance! Hurry, please!'

EPISODE 45

Logan and Hamza are sitting hand in hand on a sofa.

Hamza, to camera.

'There's been a lot of interest in our story, as you can imagine, since that show. We had a lot of requests for interviews, photoshoots. We turned all of them down.

'It's not that we were ashamed or anything. I must admit I was a little shocked – Logan hadn't discussed it with me beforehand, obviously – but then he didn't name me, he didn't actually come out of character; they could have worked it into a storyline if they'd wanted to.

'I know it would have been difficult and expensive. I'm not condoning what they did. Obviously the actors can't just take over a soap. That would be madness.

'But you know, *Market Square* had one gay character. One. Dr Anderson, the GP who lived with his partner, Jason, and was thinking about adopting a child. And it had one Muslim family, the Khans, and one black family, the Campbells, but they'd not had a good storyline for years. And this is meant to be south London. South London now, not fifty years ago. The problem with *Market Square* is that it was outdated as soon as it began.

'So now we're out as a couple, and out as individuals, and we're both unemployed. It's sort of scary. We've both enjoyed being a small part of Jake's project, because it gave us something to do.

'Our agents have been very supportive. Logan's been approached for *Strictly*. I've had some auditions. One terrorist, one extremist preacher, one pirate. I like the sound of the pirate. I'm hopeful.

'We both want to say we wish we hadn't felt the need to hide who we are. Who we love. We were scared of being stereotyped, and of people's reactions. But we shouldn't have needed to worry. We hope to prove to you that as actors we are good enough to transcend prejudice and assumptions.

'We can be anyone. We can do anything.

'So can you.'

EPISODE 46

Jake, walking along the road.

'I need to be Adam. Think my way into his head.

'He likes trains. *Thomas*, trucks, railways.

'He hates loud noise, unless it's the *Thomas* music. He doesn't like people unless they're the Fat Controller or the signalmen.

'He doesn't like crowds or noise, cars or bright lights.

'So here . . . he'd stay away from the road. He wouldn't go into the shops. He'd go onto this bit, the bit with no road, and he'd look around him for trains.

'Over there. Railway arches, old ones – I don't think the line is used anymore. They look like something from *Thomas*. He might want to hide away down there.'

Jake crosses over the road, approaches the first arch.

'Adam? Adam? Are you there?'

Jake spots a tent in a far corner.

'He'd go for that. He'd like a tent. He must be ...
Adam? Adam?'

*The tent is occupied. A man shouts at Jake, shocking
him into stumbling over.*

'OK, I'm going. I'm sorry, I'm going.'

*Jake makes off at speed. He's soon back on the main
street, trying to work out which way leads back to the
flat.*

'Everything looks the same ... we've lost Adam and
now I can't find my way home.'

*It's getting darker, and Jake's walking past some
brightly lit windows of shops and offices. He pauses at
one. It's the library.*

'They should keep these places open all night. They're
warm and there's lots to do ... you could read all night.
I mean, it's so much better than a bus. Or a tent, or a

railway bridge. A lot better than a railway bridge. Or . . .
hang on . . .

'Thomas?'

Jake's spotted a Thomas the Tank Engine *poster on
the library wall. He looks more closely. In a corner,
on a bean bag is Adam – the real Adam – looking at*
Thomas *books.*

Jake pulls out his phone.

'Mum? Mum, I found him! He's at the library. He's fine.
Can you come and get us?'

*We see Jake going into the library. He doesn't touch
Adam, or come too near. He pulls up a bean bag
and starts looking at the books scattered around
him. Adam's hand drifts towards Jake, as an
acknowledgment of his presence.*

*The brothers are so close together, and yet so far apart.
As they always have been.*

EPISODE 47

A hospital ward. Jake is sitting at Marguerite's
bedside. Marguerite is sleeping.

'I'm so sorry I left you, Marguerite. So sorry. If I'd been there, this might never have happened.

'It all went crazy at home, that's the thing. After Adam was found, you'd have thought Dad might have felt better, wouldn't you? But he fell apart. He just lay in bed, and he cried a lot, and . . .'

Jake shivers.

'I mean it's so hard to see your dad like that. You expect he's always going to be strong and, like, a leader. Someone to fight with, maybe, but not a crumpled heap in bed, who can't look after anyone or do anything or . . . '

Jake wipes away a tear.

'I suppose I'm lucky really, because at least I know how to operate in an adult world. I can talk to people much older than I am, and it doesn't bother me. So I called the lady at the BBC who said she'd help us, and they took Dad to this place, this private hospital. Mum needed to stay with Adam, so I went with him, and talked to the psychiatrist about what had happened, and talked to Dad about staying there, and then I came back home – I mean, not home, but your house, Marguerite – and you weren't there. You were here. Karoline left me a note. And I felt so bad for leaving you.

'They aren't going to prosecute Dad. It's better publicity for them if they help us, and then we won't say bad things about them. They're furious about the whole thing. Marcus sacked Kirsty and Logan on the spot, while they were still dragging Dad off the set.

'And now they've announced that *Market Square* is being closed down altogether.

'I know it wouldn't seem like much to you, Marguerite, but it's a part of people's lives. Not just the people who work there, but the viewers. People love that show. They're addicted to it. And now, because of Dad, because of me, they're losing it. It's horrible. Is everyone going to blame me?

'Please get well, Marguerite. I know you were looking for your children, that's why you fell. I'm going to try and think of a way to find them. Or find out what happened to them. Someone must know.

'Maybe I can do something on the Internet. Maybe I can put out an appeal. There must be something I can do. Something to help you.

'Something to help me as well.'

Click to see previous comments

LizzieK Sorry, I know it's a silly question but where did you film that? In a real hospital?

DestinyRock Angie called in some favours and we used the set of *Casualty*.

LizzieK I knew I recognised it!

Click to load more comments

EPISODE 48

Dame Edie Lombard as herself, in her white-walled, minimalist flat.

'Poor Marguerite.

'She married a bad one. Easy to do.

'They had two beautiful girls. I remember going to a party at their house one day in the early sixties. The girls were handing out the canapes. Sweet little things. Rosalind so fair and Sophia so dark. Hard to believe they were sisters. Of course, that didn't help.

'She had affairs, of course she did. I'm sure he did too, but he couldn't stand it. Jealousy is a terrible thing, and Marguerite's husband hated everyone who spoke to her and everything that took her away from him.

'Some men feel threatened by a woman's success. He was one of those. She realised much too late.

'He was determined to destroy her. And so he didn't just divorce her, he built a case that she was a bad mother. A terrible mother. And he took those girls away from her.

'Jake's father, there was a lot of bad feeling when he disrupted that live show. They tried to blame the end of *Market Square* on him. Jake, poor kid, took it all on his shoulders. Remember, that's why he decided to make this series in the first place. My heart was breaking when I saw his first episode.

'There are worse things that a father can do than stand up for his family. I'm not condoning what Neil Benn did, but his heart was in the right place.

'Marguerite's husband, Rosalind and Sophia's father – I'm not sure he had a heart at all. He took those children, stole them away from her. She had no idea where they were, whether they were alive, what lies they were being told about her.

'I think she had a breakdown. I know that her career pretty much ended then. She holed up in that damn house and didn't see a soul for years and years.

'I heard once that her husband had taken the girls to Canada. I also heard there was a fire, and that they were maimed, or even killed. I don't remember the details, or even when that was. Just another tragedy. Just another story.

'People laugh at series like *Market Square*, but I can tell you that life can be crueller, more shocking, more dramatic than anything seen on television. A love affair goes wrong, a job is lost, someone gets ill and things spin out of control. I've seen people go from success to utter devastation in the space of a few weeks.

'The key to strength is happiness. We take it for granted and we shouldn't. Happiness is the foundation of a good life, and if we make it central to everything we do, then love and security and success will follow. Maybe not in the way we expect, but that's the way it works.

'Jake contacted me two weeks after *Market Square* was cancelled. He came here and told me about his plan for this series. A kid like him, so young, but so determined, convinced he could turn things around. I was impressed. I was sure he would succeed.

'But when he told me about Marguerite and I realised who she was, I told him to forget about trying to find her children. "They died a long time ago," I said. "The great blessing of Alzheimer's – the one and only blessing – is that the memory of their loss has been wiped from her mind. And don't go telling her, either. She doesn't need to relive that loss again and again. Carry on reading *Hamlet* to her. Maybe she'll come to life again."'

EPISODE 49

Neil and Jake are sitting on a bench in a garden.

'Dad's been staying here for a while now. It's a specialist place for people who have problems with ... with how they're feeling.'

'You might as well say it, Jake. Mental health issues. No point hiding it.'

'I didn't know if you'd feel OK about saying it. We get quite a lot of people watching these films now.'

'Do you? I'm proud of you. Always proud of you. I never meant to ... always so proud ...'

Neil takes a long, shaky, gulping breath. Jake's arm goes round his dad's shoulders.

'I know. It's OK.'

'Who's looking after Adam, Jake? Your mum will be at work now. Who's looking after him? I'll be out of here soon. I'll be able to help, do my bit.'

'You just concentrate on getting well. It's helping, isn't it, being here?'

'I think so. They've got me taking so many pills.'

'You're doing therapy and stuff though, aren't you? Talking about how it all got too much for you.'

'I am. It does help, I feel a lot calmer.'

'They say you'll be out in a few months.'

'It's expensive, somewhere like this. It's not like the NHS. Can we actually afford this, Jake?'

'It's OK, don't worry about it. The BBC are helping, and Mum's working longer hours. Adam's going to a day centre now, Dad. This lady got in touch and she told Mum about people that could help, and now Adam goes off every day in a minibus to this place where he does stuff with other people a bit like him.'

'He doesn't like other people.'

'Not always, but there's a quiet room at the centre where he can go if he needs to. And he does seem to like lots of things there. He helps in the garden sometimes. There's a toy train track that goes round the whole of the outside space, and he loves that.'

'He would love that.'

'I thought a real train might help him talk, but it didn't.'

'It hasn't *yet*, Jake, but it might. People can change. I'm changing, I promise you that.'

'I know you are. I'm proud of you, Dad.'

There's a moment of silence. Then Jake speaks again.

'There was something you wanted to say, wasn't there, Dad?'

Neil nods. He speaks to camera.

'I just want to say, I'm sorry. I ruined your show. I should never have done that. If it wasn't for me, *Market Square* would still be on. I'm sorry, so sorry.'

Click to see previous comments

MarcusRemington As the executive editor of *Market Square*, I feel it is appropriate at this point to make some sort of comment on this web series which has become such a cultural phenomenon.

Jake, you've achieved something very special here. Millions of hits worldwide, for a show about a show – about *Market Square*, of which I was very proud. I am sorry that we decided to let you go. I truly believed we were doing you a favour. So much talent, in one so young – it would have been a crying shame to allow you to become typecast as Riley Elliott.

The decision to cast Bobby Broadbent was not mine. I'm afraid I cannot say more because I am bound by a confidentiality agreement.

It hurt a great deal to end that show. It was like ripping the heart out of a great, wounded animal, a lion or a huge bear. We had no choice after what happened. I bitterly regret it.

Market Square's success was built on the power of story. Story is part of what makes us human. From the earliest days, the art of story-telling bound us together into communities. Our shared experience is story. It is the way we make sense of our lives. Shakespeare knew that. If he were alive today he'd have been writing for *Market Square* (before it got cancelled, of course).

For those of you who are still mourning the loss of your beloved characters, I plan to put all remaining scripts and story notes online. But just to answer a few questions: Amina's wedding was going to be called off at the last minute. Stephanie did not have diabetes. Poppy was indeed going to die in childbirth, having given birth to twins.

The father of the twins was, in fact Riley – that's why we thought Jake was perhaps a little young to shoulder such a controversial storyline. Riley wasn't actually her brother after all, as it turned out that he'd been adopted.

It's very difficult for me to reveal these stories in this

blunt way, because of course they would have been played out with all the subtlety and superb writing that *Market Square* was famed for.

I'm glad to say that I'm working on a brand new project for the BBC, which we hope to announce very soon.

Click to load more comments

EPISODE 50

In a nursing home, the real Marguerite is tiny in a huge armchair.

Enter Jake and Destiny, Kirsty and Arthur, Dylan, Logan and Angie, all dressed in black. Jake sits by Marguerite's side.

'Marguerite? Can you hear me? We're here to rehearse again.

'We got a long way while you were in hospital. We've cast Angie as Gertrude, and Logan as Claudius. Arthur and Destiny are going to read Rosencrantz and Guildenstern. And Dylan, he's Polonius. He could have been Hamlet, but I nabbed it first. Alright, Dylan?'

'It's fine by me.'

'Kirsty's going to read Ophelia. So we've got everyone we need for Act 3, scene 1. Is that OK, Marguerite? You're in charge.'

Angie's doubtful. She whispers to Logan.

'The old dear's away with the fairies, if you ask me. Poor Jake.'

'It's OK, just start. You won't believe it.'

Logan speaks first.

'And can you, by no drift of circumstance,
Get from him why he puts on this confusion,
Grating so harshly all his days of quiet
With turbulent and dangerous lunacy?'

There is no response at all from Marguerite. Jake hesitates slightly and then gestures for Destiny to continue.

'He does confess he feels himself distracted;
But from what cause he will by no means speak.'

Marguerite's eyes close. Jake swallows.

251

'It always worked before. She just clicked into her old self. I can't ... it was ... you saw it, Destiny, didn't you? You saw it.'

'She's had so much change since then. She's left her home behind, all her memories there.'

'You mean you think that's it? She's lost the last bit of herself? It was all there in the house?'

'Maybe that's why she wanted to stay there.'

Dylan speaks up.

'You know, Jake, working on this, the last few weeks, rehearsing with you guys ... it's been fun. Just acting because we enjoy it. Not because it's a job, or for the money, just for enjoyment. It's been something special. It's been ... it's made me remember why I do it. And it kind of helped with the disappointment over the film ... giving it up.'

'I'm sorry.'

'It's not your fault, and I'm glad they offered it to you. But you know ... I was gutted. Angry with my parents. Just because they wanted me to concentrate on exams. This has helped.'

Kirsty's next.

'It's been good for me too. The old lady, she gave us this. Even if she can't appreciate it now.'

Angie puts her arm around Jake.

'You try, love. Let's skip forward to your bit. Maybe she'll remember your voice.'

Jake nods. His voice is uneven, flat with disappointment, as he starts to read.

'To be, or not to be: that is the question:
Whether 'tis nobler in the mind to suffer
The slings and arrows of outrageous fortune'

Marguerite's eyes snap open. She shakes her head.

'What on earth was that? Let's take it again with a little more conviction.'

Click to see previous comments

MarketSquareFan I'd like to say that I'm feeling ever so much better now. *Emmerdale* has proved to be extremely calming.
DramaticDee While I applaud your efforts to take charge of Jake's life in a time of turmoil, I would just point out that – despite his use of diverse characters – Shakespeare epitomises the Dead White Male stranglehold on Western Culture. Perhaps you will use

his new fame to explore and promote marginalised
voices in the future?

DestinyRock I certainly will. And I'll make sure Jake
does as well.

Click to load more comments

EPISODE 51

Jake in a bedroom, sitting on the bed, with Destiny and Dylan, backs against the wall. It's a very luxurious bedroom, all silk and fresh flowers.

Jake, to camera.

'You will never believe where we are.'

'Don't tell, not yet!'

'OK, Destiny, I won't tell yet. I'll just bring you up to date. We started making the web series pretty much as soon as *Market Square* was pulled. And we started showing it about eight weeks later.'

'So we were still making episodes while the first ones were showing.'

'And then come April they all did their GCSEs and I went off to Croatia to make the Prince Jasper film – which should have been Dylan's, but the filming schedule clashed with the exam period.'

'But you know, I got eight GCSEs, all top grades, while you are completely unqualified, peasant.'

'And it was great to, you know, leave everything behind. Go somewhere else and be someone else, and Croatia was really beautiful and I learned fencing and riding, and I met some amazing actors, and I felt as though I was just learning so much.'

'You don't have to go on about it.'

'And the money helped too. It helped a lot. It paid for Dad to have more treatment, and for Mum to get a carer to help with Adam.'

'And around that time – can I tell yet?'

'No, wait, Dylan. We were hoping the web series would find Marguerite's daughters, especially when it went viral. But Edie was right – they'd both died in Canada in the 1980s, in a house fire. A local historian in Alberta got in touch. We were really upset.'

'On *Market Square*, or in a film, then they'd have turned up. Just when we were putting on *Hamlet* for her. A miracle ending.'

'Yeah, Destiny, but this is real life.'

'But someone did get in touch. Her niece from Ireland. They'd lost touch with her when she moved to London and changed her name.'

'It was so sweet when she came over to meet Marguerite. She's lovely.'

'I don't think Marguerite has any idea who she is. But the most amazing thing is that she's an actress too, in Dublin, and she read some plays with Marguerite, and it was just, well . . . magic, really.'

'The house has been shut up, and it's going to be sold. Leonora – that's the niece – is talking to the lawyers about using some of the money to help homeless teenagers. People like Kayleigh. And Logan. And me.'

'Yeah and some more of it to create a scholarship to help young women who want to be theatre directors like Marguerite.'

'And you are totally going to get that scholarship, Destiny.'

'Except I might not need it. Because . . . OK, Jake, you can tell now, I can see you are bursting—'

'We are in Hollywood!'

'Hollywood!'

'It's totally true!'

Short clip showing the hotel room – actually a hotel suite – and palm trees from the window.

'Basically, Zoe got a call. Simon Steinberg wants to take the web series and adapt it into a movie.'

'It's all thanks to Dylan. Simon Steinberg started watching it because of him.'

'They're going to Americanise it, obviously. Set it in New York. Noah Blaskett's probably going to play me.'

'Don't you mind that, Jake?'

'I did at first. But then I realised how weird it would be to play an American version of me in a film about making a web series about my actual real life.'

'Simon said he wants me to play Adam. Are you sure you're alright with that?'

'I'd rather it was you than anyone else, Dylan. You did a great job.'

'So we're here to meet the executive producers and sign the contracts, and it's just awesome and amazing and brilliant and I can't quite believe it.'

'It may never happen. Zoe says sometimes these things just never get made.'

'We still get some money though. And you've got Prince Jasper coming out next year.'

'Yeah, and there's more actually . . . '

'More?'

Jake swallows. He's trying to hide how excited he is.

'I've been getting calls about live theatre, about actually performing *Hamlet* on stage.'

'No! Really?'

'You want to do that, Jake?'

'More than anything, because it'll be different every

time. You're creating something new every single night you play the part.'

'And it won't matter that the money's crap because ... Hollywood!'

'Yeah, Hollywood!'

'So, here we are, in a big Hollywood suite ... '

'I've got a room next door. I'm not sharing with these two—'

'And it feels like a good place to end.'

'To end?'

'The web series. We're sort of done now.'

'But there's stuff we haven't covered yet! Like you making up with Orson.'

'He won't do it. He said sorry, and so did I and we're fine now, but it was on the basis that I don't talk about it in public. So I've already probably said too much.'

'You don't have to live your whole life in public.'

'No. I think it's time to be a bit more private.'

'So you're not going to show us round your beautiful new home?'

'Not with cameras. And it's nothing special, anyway. Just a studio flat near Mum and Adam, so I can help out but not have to share a room.'

'You really like it though, don't you?'

'If I hadn't spent all those months sleeping on sofas and futons and floors and buses, I wouldn't think that much of it. But now, having a bed and a bookshelf, a desk and a bathroom – it's just everything I need. I can read and rehearse and think. You don't realise how much you need a home until you don't have one anymore.'

'Don't you get lonely?'

'Not so far. I have so many people in my head – so many parts to think about – that I need time on my own, just to remember who I am. And I go and see Mum and Adam and Marguerite and everyone, and I'm doing acting courses too. It's fine. It's good.'

'So, this is it really, isn't it? The end of the web series?'

'I think so, don't you? We can't go on and on and on . . .'

'It's not a soap, after all.'

'We could leave it open though, couldn't we? Just in case we have stuff to announce.'

'Or something big happens.'

'Even bigger than Hollywood!'

'I suppose we could say this is the end, but it isn't really.'

'Just goodbye for now.'

'You never know when we'll be back.'

'Thank you for watching.'

All three together:

'Bye!'

ACKNOWLEDGMENTS:

A huge thank you to three inspiring men: Charlie Rowe, who told me about life as a young actor, Simon Binns, who shared his experience of homelessness and working with homeless people at the YMCA hostel in Crouch End, north London, and David Savill, director of Age Exchange, an arts organisation which works with people with dementia. Marguerite's story was based on their work.

I was awarded an Arts Council grant to help me research and write *Cuckoo*, for which I am everlastingly grateful.

Thank you to my wonderful agent, Jenny Savill and all at ANA. Thanks to the brilliant team at Atom, James, Olivia, Emma, Stephie, Kate and Rachel and especially my editor Sarah Castleton, who took on all my strange ideas about a book that wasn't really a book and made sense of them. And thank you to Jack Smyth for a truly great cover.

Thank you to Kate and Noa, the brilliant librarians at the Highgate Wood School LRC, and the Y7 and Y8 reading groups, who gave me valuable feedback.

Thank you to Jack Jewers, maker of the brilliant Night School web series, for his film-making expertise, and to Denise Lester and Dennis Sharpe for telling me about the law regarding children and parents and money.

Thank you to all my friends, and especially those who read and discussed *Cuckoo*: Fiona Dunbar, Valerie Kampmeier, Susie Day, Sophia Bennett, Keris Stainton, Lee Weatherly, Nic Hardstaff, Jo Williams and Greg Ashton. Thank you to Emma and Roger for lending me your flat for a crucial week of writing.

Thank you to Andy and Wendy Barnes and Paul Herbert, for getting me interested in writing scripts in the first place.

Thank you to my family, and most of all to Laurence, Phoebe and Judah. You are the best.